The
Diddakoi

Rumer Godden

MACMILLAN CHILDREN'S BOOKS

For Emma

First published 1972 by Macmillan Children's Books

This edition published 2013 by Macmillan Children's Books
an imprint of Pan Macmillan
The Smithson, 6 Briset Street, London EC1M 5NR
Associated companies throughout the world
www.panmacmillan.com

ISBN 978-0-230-76989-2

7 9 8 6

A CIP catalogue record for this book is available from the British Library.

Typeset by Intype Libra Ltd
Printed and bound by CPI Group (UK) Ltd, Croydon CR0 4YY

MIX
Paper from
responsible sources
FSC® C116313

Foreword

Before writing *The Diddakoi* Rumer Godden did a great deal of reading and research. For all her books, whether about India or ballet or dogs – especially Pekinese dogs (her favourites) – she spent time delving deeply into the subject. The facts must, she knew, be right, and one important fact with this book concerned the title. The actual word Diddakoi is explained very early on; and we find that it describes someone who is half Gypsy and half of Irish background, exactly like Kizzy, the central character.

Kizzy is a passionate, high-spirited girl who fights against injustice, unfairness and cruelty as her upbringing has taught her. Rumer Godden frequently wrote about characters who felt different and found it hard to fit into an expected pattern. She would say that they were very like herself.

Rumer Godden was born in Sussex in 1907, the second of four daughters, and she lived for much of her childhood in India, in Narayanganj, East Bengal, which is now Bangladesh. Her father worked for the Brahmaputra River Steam Navigation Company, and she and her sisters were happy with little formal schooling, enjoying the colourful life close to the river.

From an early age she started writing stories and

poems, hiding them secretly in the hollow of the large cork tree outside the family house. When she was only ten, she secretly sent a story to a newspaper and to her family's surprise – and her own – it was published.

She always thought of herself as different – the odd one out . . . the outsider – and her behaviour at home, and later when she was sent to school in England, could be difficult. When she was in her teens, a strict but very understanding teacher realized that she had the makings of a writer, and guided her in the right directions.

Rumer never forgot this teacher and I think she may have been the inspiration behind some of the wonderfully sympathetic adult characters in her stories about children. In *The Diddakoi*, especially, the wise characters of Olivia Brooke, Admiral Twiss and his manservant, Peters, come to mind.

The Diddakoi was first published in 1972, and Rumer Godden was extremely surprised when a message arrived telling her that the book had won the Children's Books category of the Whitbread Award for that year. One of the judges was the famous and popular author Kingsley Amis, and on praising *The Diddakoi* he added that he wished some books for adults were as well written.

Four years later there was a dramatization of it on BBC Television, called *Kizzy*, which introduced many new readers to the book.

Like other books by Rumer Godden *The Diddakoi* immediately suggests characters and situations that come to life *off the page*. Her books have been adapted for film, radio and theatre, and I first came to know her when I wanted to use extracts from one story for an anthology of scenes for young drama students. She was pleased about this and, as we talked, I felt privileged to discover her great love of storytelling.

Reading *The Diddakoi* again this year I found myself caught up anew in the events – feeling sad all over again at the death of Kizzy's grandmother; feeling angry at the way the village children bullied her, led by the spoilt little horror Prudence Cuthbert.

It is one of the most memorable stories, with its changing scenes and situations, lively dialogue, tensions and fears, and especially in its bringing together of a group of people who need each other.

Rumer Godden died in 1998, and I think she would have been pleased with this new edition of *The Diddakoi*, over forty years after it was first published.

Anne Harvey

Chapter One

Diddakoi.
Tinker.
Tinkety-tink.
Gypsy, gypsy joker, get a red hot poker.
Rags an' tags.
Clothes pegs. Who'll buy my clothes-pegs?
– only they said 'cloes-pegs'.
Who'll buy my flowers?
– only they said 'flahrs'.
Diddakoi.

'If anyone,' said the teacher, Mrs Blount, in the class-room, 'any *one*,' and her eyes looked sternly along the lines of tables filled with boys and girls, 'teases or bullies or jeers at Kizzy Lovell, they will answer for it to me.'

Twenty-eight pairs of eyes looked back at Mrs Blount blandly and innocently: 'As if we would,' they seemed to say. The twenty-ninth pair, Kizzy's, looked down at her table; she had a curious burning in her ears.

1

'To me,' said Mrs Blount. 'We shall not have such behaviour in this school.' But they would; silent and small, Kizzy knew that.

'Kizzy must be short for something.' Mrs Blount had asked her, 'What is your real name, dear?'

'Kizzy.'

Mrs Blount had touched a sore spot; in Kizzy's family, as in some gypsy clans, a child is given three names: a secret one whispered by its mother the moment it is born and, when it is grown, whispered again into the child's ear; a private or 'wagon' name which is used only by its own people, and a third open name by which it is known to the world. Kizzy seemed only to have one, but that was because she was what they called her, a 'diddakoi', not all gypsy. 'We don't say gypsies now. We say travellers,' Mrs Blount told the children. Kizzy's father, pure Rom, had married an Irish girl, but Kizzy looked gypsy to the children and they were half fascinated, half repelled by her brownness and the little gold rings in her ears – none of the other girls had golden earrings. There was one boy Kizzy liked, big Clem Oliver. 'I thought gypsies had black eyes,' said Clem Oliver. 'Yours are dark dark brown. They're nice – and these are pretty.' He touched the gold rings and Kizzy glowed and, 'My Gran has gold sov'reigns for her earrings,' she told Clem.

'Never seen sov'reigns,' said Clem in awe. Clem made Kizzy feel bigger, not small and frightened, big an' warm, thought Kizzy. Clem, though, was in an older class; she only saw him at break times, and the others teased. 'More than teased,' said Mrs Blount.

'But, Mildred, if you forbid people to do something, doesn't it usually make them want to do it even more?' asked Miss Olivia Brooke. Pretty Mrs Blount – Mildred – and her husband, the young Welfare Officer, Mr Blount, who had brought Kizzy to school, were lodging with Miss Brooke in the village until their own new house was built and had told her about Kizzy. 'Doesn't it?' asked Miss Brooke.

'These are *children*.'

'Children are people, Mildred.'

'Well, what would you have done?' Mrs Blount's voice was high; she did not like being told about children; after all, she was college-trained.

'Could you, perhaps, have interested them in the little girl? Made her romantic. Gypsies—'

'Travellers,' corrected Mrs Blount.

'I like the old name. Gypsies have a romantic side. If, perhaps, you had told them stories . . .' but Mrs Blount said she preferred to use her own methods and, 'I want you to give me your promise,' she told the class, 'that there will be no more teasing of Kizzy,' and she even asked them, child by child, 'Do you promise?'

'Mary Jo, do you promise?'

'Yes, Mrs Blount.'

'Prudence Cuthbert, do you?'

3

'Yes, Mrs Blount,' said Prue.

'Yes, Mrs Blount . . . Yes, Mrs Blount,' the answers came back, glib and meek – what Mrs Blount did not know was that every girl said it with her fingers crossed. Kizzy saw that from her seat at the back of the room and knew, as soon as Mrs Blount was out of the way, it would start again. *Tinker . . . diddakoi . . . gypsy joker . . . clothes pegs . . . old clothes . . .*

Kizzy had come to school in new clothes, or thought she had. Unlike traveller men who often order fancy suits, traveller women seldom buy new clothes from shops; they make them or beg them or buy them at country jumble sales, but hers had looked to Kizzy brand new; she loved the tartan skirt and red jersey, the school blue blazer all of them wore, white socks, but, 'Wearing Prue Cuthbert's clothes,' the girls jeered.

'They're mine,' said Kizzy.

'Now. They were Prue's. Prue's mum gave them for you.' Prudence Cuthbert was the worst of the girls and that night Kizzy had put the clothes down a hollow in one of the old apple trees in the orchard, a hollow full of dead leaves and water. Her grandmother had lammed her but Kizzy did not care; no one could wear them after that, and next day she wore her own clothes for school. It had never occurred to her, or her Gran, that they were peculiar clothes, but they looked most peculiar in class: a limp strawberry-pink cotton dress too long for her – her

4

vest showed at the top – a brown cardigan that had been a boy's larger than Kizzy, but if she pushed the sleeves up it was not much too big; some of the buttons had come off but Gran had found two large safety-pins. Kizzy wore gumboots over bare legs – she had washed the boots, not her legs, but mud still clung to them. 'Where's your coat?' asked Mrs Blount.

'Don't need a coat.' Kizzy said it gruffly because she did not have a coat and was afraid someone would give her one. She spoiled the look of the school, 'and those clothes smell,' said Prudence, wrinkling up her pretty white nose. They did, but not of dirt. Gran washed them often, hanging them along the hedge, while Kizzy wrapped herself in a blanket; they smelled of the open air, of wood-smoke and a little of the old horse, Joe, because she often hugged him.

'You live in a caravan?' asked Prue and, for the first time, she sounded interested.

'In a wagon,' said Kizzy.

'It's a caravan. I seen it.'

'A wagon,' said Kizzy.

'In Admiral Twiss's orchard. He lets you but he's barmy.'

'He's not,' said Kizzy.

'He is. Everybody knows it. Barmy. Nuts.'

Prudence doubled up. Kizzy's hard small fist, hard as any boy's, had hit her in the middle of her stomach.

★

He was Admiral Sir Archibald Cunningham Twiss but everyone called him Admiral Twiss – except his man, Peters, and Nat, the groom, who said 'Admiral Sir'; Kizzy, in her own mind, called him 'Sir Admiral'. He lived in the great house of the village, Amberhurst House, as all his family had before him. 'But they kept a proper big house,' said the villagers. 'Servants and footmen, a coachman, grooms and gardeners.' Now there were only Admiral Twiss's man, Peters, who had been with him in the Navy, and Nat, the bow-legged groom. 'Not a woman near the place,' said the village.

'Thanks be,' said Peters. Neither he nor Nat held with women and the Admiral was shy of them, shy and wary. 'Don't trust 'em,' said Admiral Twiss.

To see Amberhurst village from the Downs was like looking at a map. 'Why are they called "downs" when they're up?' asked Kizzy. The hills ran green and chalky to the horizon, the valley wide below; the village did not nestle in it, but stood up clear and plain, its short street leading to the common where a jumble of cottages edged the green. Miss Brooke's cottage was the last on the common. The Cuthberts' new white house stood out at the top of the village street; then came the garage, a market garden, the post office–bakery shop. The Council estate, with the school on its far side, spread back almost to Amber-hurst woods and the House park with its old chestnut trees. The church had once been part of the park but had its own plot and drive now. The House still crowned the knoll; its yew walk, the lawns and walled kitchen garden could be seen from the Downs with the stables behind; they had a cupola with a clock and, above the hayloft, a weathercock that, in sunshine, glinted for miles. An avenue of lime trees led to the tall gates where Nat lived alone in the lodge. Though the grass was creeping up to the huge stone house, 'and the bell pull often comes off in your hand if you ring it,' said Mrs Cuthbert, the Admiral still let the villagers play cricket in the grounds and the pitch was kept rolled and smooth, and there were still horses, high-bred yearlings and two-year-olds at grass in the paddocks. 'Then they goes to be trained,' said Nat.

Admiral Twiss was long and thin with fierce eyes and eyebrows and moustaches that seemed to the village children to bristle at them, but his hands, that were fine and thin too, were gentle – as any of his horses could have told – and deft. He made models, chiefly of ships, sometimes sail, sometimes steam; he never spoke to the village children, nor they to him – they were afraid of the eyebrows and moustaches – but he made a model church, big enough for a child to creep into, and every Christmas stood it at the House gates. The church was lit up so that its stained-glass windows shone, every tiny piece perfect, and from inside came music, carols that Kizzy liked to think were tiny people singing – Prudence would have told her at once it was a tape – and at midday and midnight, bells would ring a miniature carillon.

In the wagon Kizzy could hear them and knew it was Christmas. Admiral Twiss, too, always sent Kizzy's Gran a cockerel for Christmas, some oranges and dates, and a bag of oats for Joe. Sometimes Kizzy thought the oranges and dates were for her; sometimes she thought the Admiral did not know that she existed.

He used to come down at sunset and stand looking at his horses just before Nat took them in; they came to the Admiral for sugar and Kizzy used to hide behind the wagon wheels to watch. If he saw Gran he would lift his tweed hat and say, 'Good evening, Mrs Lovell.' He never called her 'Granny', 'as some do,' said Gran, and spat. 'He has manners.'

He had put aside the orchard for the travellers and laid on water, a tap and a trough for them, though the village did not approve. 'It's my land,' said Admiral Twiss. 'They don't do any harm,' – in the orchard they kept his rule of no litter – 'Besides, they like my horses.' The paddocks ran along the back of the orchard where, on the other side of the hedge, the gypsies' rough horses used to be tethered; they were gone now; the caravans were towed by cars or lorries or were mechanized themselves.

The only horse was Gran's and Kizzy's Joe, who was the last of the many horses who had once drawn the wagon, plodding along the roads to meadows and commons all over England, grazing on the road verges where, though even then there was plenty of traffic, the grass was still sweet, not so petrol-tainted and strewn with litter, and travellers could pull in to camp almost anywhere if the farmers and landowners were willing. 'There was smoke in the lanes then,' Gran used to say, from many a campfire. The horses spent the winter with the family in some site like the Admiral's, coming close to the campfire that smelt of apple or cherry wood branches to get warm, and had, like most of the humans, a sack across their backs. Joe was the only one left now – most of the sites set apart for travellers would not let a horse in – but Joe still grazed close to his wagon, which was one of the few horse-caravans still lived in. Though its wheels were rotten and its axles rusty so that it could not be moved, its paint shabby, the brass was still bright, the lace curtains at its windows stiff with starch; it was gay with Gran's good china and photographs, a bunch of plastic roses Kizzy had bought for her, saucepans and a frying pan. Kizzy had been born in the wagon.

'Does your mother wash?' they asked her at school. If she had said 'Yes', Kizzy knew they would say, 'She's a washerwoman'; if she answered 'No', they said, 'Then she's a dirty sow', but Kizzy did not have to say either; her mother was dead, and her father. 'Who d'you live with then?'

'I live with my Gran.'

Gran was not Kizzy's Gran but her Gran-Gran-

9

Gran, her great-great-grandmother. If she had told that to the children at school, they might have been impressed, but Kizzy told nothing, not to Gran about school, nor at school about Gran who might have been a hundred. 'Yes, perhaps a hundred years old,' Mr Blount told his wife and Miss Brooke. 'A true old-fashioned traveller.' Gran smoked a clay pipe; her face was dark and wrinkled by wind and fire smoke, as were her clothes; she had long ago lost her teeth, 'but it's a fine proud face,' said Mr Blount. 'They say she's lived there in Admiral Twiss's orchard for the past twenty years, perhaps more.'

Living alone with her Gran, some of those hundred years had rubbed off on Kizzy, who seemed far older than her size. It was Kizzy who took the shabby bag to Rye, the small nearby town, for shopping, Kizzy who went to the corn merchants to beg the spillings out of the bins or sacks for Joe – even if Gran and Kizzy went short, the old horse had corn in his nosebag once a day and, if Gran could get beer, she gave half to him. In spring Gran warmed bunches of pussy willow at the fire to make the buds come out and Kizzy took them, not to the village but to Rye, and sold them from house to house: palm and the first sticky-buds. Gran made baskets of willow twigs that bend easily and planted the baskets with primrose roots in moss and Kizzy sold those too; they were so dainty people would buy them – and perhaps Kizzy's brown eyes that Clem Oliver liked made a difference. In winter she sold mistletoe and holly.

Gran could not make holly wreaths now, her hands were too shaky, Kizzy's too small, but they lived happily in the orchard. Gran kept the caravan while Kizzy was away and went stick-gathering for the fire they lit and kept protected by a shelter of two sheets of corrugated iron, with sacks to keep out the wind. No one could build a fire like Gran; she sat on a bench, a plank across two piles of bricks; Kizzy had a fish-box that had *McPhail and Son, Aberdeen* stencilled on its side, but it was sturdy, the right size for Kizzy, and when it grew warm from the heat of the fire it gave out a sweet resin smell. They would eat their breakfast or supper there, sometimes a stew, but more often nowadays bread and butter, perhaps a spread of dripping. Kizzy's grandfather and father would have snared rabbits, sometimes a hare, even a pheasant to put in the pot; she had a dim remembrance of eating hedgehog – 'hotchi-witchi' Gran called it – but they had to manage without such things now though sometimes they had pan cake – cake fried in the frying pan. The black kettle sang on its hook, Gran's kittle-iron, and presently they would have a mug of strong tea, drinking it in the firelight, their backs protected with a sack and Joe tearing up grass, keeping as close to them as he could get.

Kizzy did not have toys, except an old skipping-rope that Gran had bought with some jumble – travellers are forever buying and selling things. Kizzy did not need toys when she had Joe. She combed him with an old curry-comb and brushed his mane and tail; she would sit beside him in the grass, giving him buttercups, of which he was fond; if she lay down beside him he would sometimes push her with his nose; the breath from his nostrils was warm, and now and again he would gently lick her face. A horse's lick is clean to a traveller. 'Well, they only drinks clean water,' Gran said. 'Not like dogs' – travellers keep their dogs apart – 'Not let come into the wagons like "they" lets 'em into rooms – covering everything in hair.' To Gran, 'they' were 'gorgios', people who were not gypsy. Gran had no dog now, but Joe moved his big hairy feet carefully round the campfire, always coming to see what they had for supper, always getting a crust of bread. Sometimes Kizzy climbed on the fence and called him and got on his back; it was so broad she could lie down there too and feel him swaying, rippling his muscles as he moved, munching, across the grass. When the apples were ripe she would stand up on his back and reach him an apple; Admiral Twiss would not mind: he kept apples in his pockets for his own satin-skinned colts and fillies. They were beautiful, 'Yet I wouldn' change you,' Kizzy whispered to Joe, 'not ever.' But there is never an 'ever'; that February, getting off the bus, Kizzy had had two bunches of early palm and catkins left; Prudence Cuthbert's house was near the bus stop and Kizzy had knocked at the back door. She only wanted to sell her bunches; she had not met Mrs Cuthbert then – nor Prue.

Mrs Cuthbert was a busy lady, busy doing good to people, 'whether they likes it or not,' said the Admiral's Peters. He knew Mrs Cuthbert well: 'Always coming to the front door to ask for this or that: flowers for the altar, vegetables for the Women's Institute stall. Would Sir Archibald open the gardens for the Horticultural Society Week?' 'Nothing to see,' said Peters. 'Will he lend the park for the Fête?' 'An' upset the horses,' said Nat, 'and ruin the cricket pitch,' said Peters. 'The village would thank you for that.' 'Will you do this, do that, lend this, give that?' mocked Peters. Mrs Cuthbert was a churchwarden and on the PCC (the Parochial Church Council). She was on the School Board, in the WI and the WVS. 'Wouldn't it be better, my dear,' Mr Cuthbert, Prudence's father, had once asked, 'to – er – work for one thing at a time?' Mrs Cuthbert managed to work for them all, and the NSPCC, and the RSPCA. 'RIP. That's what I wish,' said Peters, which is usually said when people are dead. 'Hush. She means well,' said Admiral Twiss.

Mrs Cuthbert had opened the door to Kizzy and when Kizzy saw her white overall, her neatly-banded fair hair and the sparklingly clean kitchen beyond, she had nearly turned tail. She had half expected Mrs Cuthbert to say, as many people did, 'No gypsies,' but

13

Mrs Cuthbert would never have said that; instead her blue eyes looked Kizzy over and, 'You ought to be in school,' she said.

Kizzy mutely held up her bunches but Mrs Cuthbert was not to be deflected. 'Why are you not in school?'

'Because I don't go to school,' but Kizzy did not say it. She said nothing, only offered her bunches.

Mrs Cuthbert had not bought one. She gave Kizzy a piece of delicious hot gingerbread – she was an excellent cook – but she had still asked questions.

'How old are you? You must be six or seven.'

Kizzy did not know. Gran always said such things were not important. 'You're as old as you are,' said Gran, and that was the answer Kizzy innocently gave, 'I'm as old as I am.'

To her surprise Mrs Cuthbert seemed to swell like a puff adder – Kizzy had seen adders. 'You're an impertinent little girl!' she said with venom and shut the door.

She must have told about Kizzy; two days later Mr Blount had come to the orchard with a Schools Inspector and asked the same question – gorgios, Kizzy was to find, continuously asked questions. 'But surely you know how old she is,' the Inspector had said.

'She must have been registered when she was born,' said Mr Blount.

'Don't hold with such things,' said Gran.

'When's your birthday, then?' they asked Kizzy at school. Mrs Blount wrote the class birthdays down on the calendar; a boy had a buttonhole, a girl a wreath of flowers, and the others marched round them singing 'Happy birthday to you,' but there was another side to birthdays Mrs Blount did not know; the girls got you by your arms and legs and bumped you on the asphalt playground, once for every year, and they pulled your hair for the number of them with extra tugs 'to make your hair grow,' and 'for luck'. Kizzy could not say when her birthday was because she did not know – it had never occurred to her and Gran that people had them. 'Well, we'd better bump you every day in case we miss it,' said Prue, but they did not like to touch her dirty boots so they tugged her hair instead, handfuls of her mop of dark curls. Kizzy had red patches on her scalp every day now and they ached at night: 'Why didn't you just say a day?' said Clem Oliver.

'I don't know a day.'

'Any day would do,' suggested Clem. 'You could pretend,' but Kizzy did not know how to pretend. Since she had come to school, she sometimes thought she did not know anything. For instance, she was not used to sitting on a chair – there was a chair in the wagon but that was Gran's – and the hours in the classroom seemed long and stuffy to her. Then there was the loo: 'I'm not going to sit on that!' Kizzy had cried when Mrs Blount showed it to her.

'But Admiral Twiss built you a privy in the orchard,' said Mrs Blount.

'It hadn't water.' Kizzy had gasped when Mrs Blount pulled the plug with its terrifying gush, 'And I didn't like that either.'

'So?'

'I walked off,' said Kizzy, which was a traveller's way of saying she went apart and did it behind a bush.

Kizzy walked off at school, among the gooseberry bushes, and Prudence caught her.

Then Mrs Blount had to insist on Kizzy using the loo and Prudence, creeping up to spy – Kizzy had not realized she could lock the door – found her sitting face to the wall and called the other girls to look. 'Think you're sittin' on a horse?' they jeered.

When Kizzy could not bear it any more she ran home. There was a hole in the playground hedge; the hedge was holly and the prickles tore but Kizzy got through to save being seen going out of the gate; then, her dress more ragged than ever, her hot cheeks scratched, her curly hair full of holly leaves, she ran down the lane, her old boots splashing in the puddles, until she reached home, the wagon in the orchard and Gran: the wagon, Gran and Joe – Joe – Joe. Mrs Blount let her go but Kizzy always knew that in the morning she would have to go back.

'Admiral Twiss sends his compliments and I have come for the little girl.'

It was a cold March afternoon with flurries of snow outside the window, but the classroom was warm and the children had been quietly, almost sleepily, painting in their places; every head jerked wide awake when Peters came stumping in.

Peters was so short and small he was like a barrel on short legs; neither he nor Nat, who had been a jockey and seemed to be made of wire covered with old parched leather, reached to the Admiral's shoulder. 'Twiss's two gnomes,' the Doctor and Vicar called them and, like gnomes, invisible for all the village saw of them, they tended him. No one would have guessed Peters had been in the Navy, except that he liked things 'shipshape' as he said; he was a dapper little man with a fresh rosy complexion and country blue eyes. He walked with a roll but that was because he had a bad leg. 'Shot in a battle,' the village boys liked to think but it had been crushed in a train accident; nor was he tattooed but not even Clem could say Peters was not a proper sailor.

The boys and girls gazed at Peters as he handed Mrs Blount a note. 'Mr Fraser told me, Ma'am, to give you this.' Mr Fraser was the headmaster. When she had read it Mrs Blount got up and came down through the tables to Kizzy Lovell, bent and put an arm round her. 'Kizzy,' she said gently, 'you are to go with Mr Peters,' and when Peters had taken Kizzy away, Mrs Blount told the children that Kizzy's grandmother was dead.

Admiral Twiss had found her late that morning lying underneath the wagon and had guessed at once what had happened. Travellers are laid in the open air when they are dying; they do not like to die inside, not even in their wagons; and Gran was peaceful on the frozen grass with Joe quietly cropping tufts alongside. The Admiral had called Nat and they carried her into the wagon and laid her carefully on her bunk; then Nat had gone to find the Smiths and Does, travellers the Admiral knew were in a camp not far away – the Does were Gran's cousins' cousins. Admiral Twiss had stayed with Gran until the Does' lorry and trailer came bumping in to the orchard; the Smiths were not far behind. They built a fire and made a strong brew of tea; he drank a cup with them, then walked up to the House with Lumas Doe to telephone the doctor and find a letter the Admiral had written long ago at Gran's dictation and kept for her. 'So they will know what to do,' she had said. He gave the letter to Lumas. It was only then that they had thought of Kizzy.

When Peters led her out of school, a woman was waiting at the gate. Kizzy knew her, she was Mrs Doe. 'Wouldn't come in,' said Peters. She took Kizzy's hand and Peters drove them away in the Admiral's ancient Rolls-Royce.

'A Rolls-Royce!' said Clem.

'A very old Rolls,' said Prue.

Chapter Two

'What shall we do with Kizzy?'

It was two days later, the evening of Gran's funeral, and they had just had supper in the orchard: Lumas and Mrs Doe, their fourteen-year-old twins and their son Boyo, the two Smiths, the Smiths' grown-up son, his wife and baby, old, old Uncle Jess and Kizzy were gathered round the fire, drinking mugs of tea. The fire was large and sent sparks up into the sky. Joe made a dark shape at the end of the orchard; he seemed to want to keep away from the motor caravan, the trailer and lorry, and occasionally blew through his nostrils as if he did not like the smell of them, or having all these people in his orchard, and shook his head.

Kizzy sat on the ground, her chin on her knees so that the brown cardigan could cover them, her arms round them. 'Give Boyo your box,' Mrs Doe had commanded. 'He's got a cold coming on and mustn't sit on the ground.' 'You're making a fool of that boy,' said Uncle Jess, but Mrs Doe took no notice and without a word Kizzy had got up and let the big heavy boy in his thick corduroy breeches have her

19

warm place. Mrs Smith – she had told Kizzy to call her Aunt Em – made room for her on the plank bench, but Kizzy sat on the ground; she seemed smaller like that and perhaps if she were out of sight they would forget her. If they did she could live perfectly well in the orchard with Joe and the wagon; if they would all just go away, but they went on talking over her head.

'Wish we could take her,' said Mrs Smith.

'We could *but* . . .' said Mrs Doe, and the 'but' seemed to fill the whole orchard.

'Should be no argument,' said Uncle Jess. 'Even if they're not our family, our children stay with us.'

'All very well for you to talk,' Mrs Smith and Mrs Doe said together. ''Tisn't you as does it.'

The lights from the trailers threw bright circles on the grass, brighter than any lights had been in the orchard for a long time; Gran had had an oil lamp with an old pink shade, but now the wagon stood apart and unlit. 'We'll see to that at midnight,' said Mrs Doe. 'Don't want no snoopers.'

'They won't be out tonight,' said Mr Smith. 'Far too cold,' and indeed more snow was falling. The fire was hot on Kizzy's face, the twigs and branches crackled cheerfully, but her back was cold; she was cold inside too, with a fear that was growing. If only they would go away.

The wagon was almost empty; Mrs Doe had taken Kizzy's bedding and put it in one of their tents with

Boyo. 'You can sleep here.' Kizzy had protested. 'I want to sleep in our own wagon.'

'Hush,' said Aunt Em Smith. 'No one can sleep there.'

'Why *not*?'

'For one thing your Gran left her orders.' For another, though Mrs Smith did not say it, many true travellers will not use anything belonging to the dead; besides, there were Gran's wishes. 'Doesn't do to go against the dead,' yet there was Mrs Doe arguing about Gran's china.

'It's mine too,' said Kizzy, but no one listened.

'Old Crown Derby, that's what it is,' declared Mrs Doe. 'Might be worth a mint.'

'Us must smash it.'

'Nonsense, Em. Prob'ly ten pounds a cup and saucer.'

'Us must.'

'That's old thinking.' Mrs Doe was scornful. 'Look, you take half and I'll take half.'

'Why, if I took any of that into the trailer, I should be feart!' said Mrs Smith. 'To begin with, Uncle Jess would have a fit.'

'Uncle! He's old. 'Course he thinks like that, but why bother about him?' Mrs Doe's voice was shrill. 'Come on, Em. You can have first pick,' but Mrs Smith shook her head and backed away. 'Well, please yourself,' and Mrs Doe took the china, the mirror, even the vase of plastic flowers into her caravan. 'The

21

fry pan's good,' she took that too. So I can't make pan cake, thought Kizzy, but the old bucket and saucepans were left. I can manage with those. Gran, in the letter, had not mentioned Kizzy. ''Course not,' said Uncle Jess. 'Her took it for granted.'

Uncle Jess was a Smith, an old old man, almost as old as Gran; he lived and travelled with his Smith grandson's family and had no wagon or trailer of his own. 'If I had, things would be different,' said Uncle Jess.

'Now Uncle,' said Mrs Smith. The Smiths had Uncle Jess, their son, his wife and baby and just one trailer and a small tent, while the Does were moving into a council house. 'Settling,' said Uncle Jess in disdain, 'going in brick!'

'It's for school,' said Mrs Doe. 'Boyo must go to school – and the girls, of course. The Council don't like overcrowding – and it isn't children,' she added under Uncle Jess's scornful eye, ''tisn't children as are the bother. When they could just be let run, one child more or less didn't matter. These days, it's the things they have to have.'

Kizzy raised her head. 'I don't want any things.'

''Tisn't what you want, dearie,' said Mrs Smith. 'It's what they say you have to have – uniforms.' Uncle Jess snorted. 'They do, Uncle – blazers at least and shoes and satchels.'

'Bathing things, a towel, and I don't know what,' said Mrs Doe. 'Then it's ten pence for this, ten pence

22

for that. I tell you it's hard enough to afford it for the three we have,' said Mrs Doe. 'Wish we could manage to take Kizzy, but we can't. She goes to school here – they'll find her a foster home.'

Always 'they', 'they', thought Kizzy. 'They' were against gypsies.

'No child of ours,' said Uncle Jess, 'was ever took into care.'

'She isn't ours. She's half gorgio,' and, 'Things are different now,' said Mrs Doe again.

'Queer,' said Uncle Jess. 'When you had one wagon there was plenty of room; in a fine house with three bedrooms there's no room at all.'

'P'raps when she's older . . .' said Mrs Doe.

'She'll take up more room,' said Uncle Jess.

'Give over, Uncle, do,' said Mrs Smith.

'I tells you, we must take the child,' said Uncle Jess, speaking directly to Lumas Doe. 'When I says we, I means you.'

'You shut your mouth,' said Mrs Doe.

'Are you goin' to let your 'ooman talk to me like that?' Uncle Jess asked quietly of Lumas Doe, but Lumas only shrugged. 'And you a man,' said Uncle Jess and spat. 'Things a'nt what they used to be,' said Uncle.

Kizzy was too tired to follow more; in any case she was not going with any of them, or anywhere. She would stay in the orchard in her own wagon no matter what Aunt Em said, in her own wagon with Joe

23

and soon, in spite of the coldness of the frozen ground, she fell asleep. In her dream she thought she heard Joe trampling and a great roaring noise and she woke with a start. The fire seemed enormous and bright; it was the men trampling, not Joe. Kizzy stumbled to her feet and Mrs Smith caught her by the shoulders. 'It's all right, darlin'. You stay here with me,' but Kizzy was standing transfixed.

Flames were rushing up in the orchard, so bright they seemed to be dancing in the apple trees and so hot they seemed to scorch Kizzy's face. A trail of sparks streamed over the paddocks; it was as well that the young horses were in the stables at night. 'Fire's too high,' said Lumas. 'It'll wake the Admiral up and summun'll come down on us. Ring the police or fire brigade or Lord knows what.' The Admiral had woken but, 'They know what they're doing,' the Admiral said to himself, turned over and went to sleep.

Joe, like Kizzy, seemed transfixed. There was a smell of burning paint and wood and hot metal; the men walked round the great fire, poking it with poles. They were burning the wagon; as Kizzy watched, the body sank, came away from the wheels and the roof fell in. 'But why?' asked Kizzy. 'Why?'

The words seemed to be wrung out of her, but they were quiet. Mrs Smith knelt down beside her and Kizzy smelled her comforting traveller smell, wood smoke and old clothes, but all the same she did not lean against Aunt Em. 'See, love, your Gran was an old-fashioned Romany and they, when they die, lays down that their wagon is to be burnt and all they things – yes, rightly, the china smashed up and ornaments and that – they clothes and photographs burned. We don't do it now, leastways most of us don't, but your Gran wanted it and we promised.' She looked at Kizzy's face. 'Your Gran wanted it, sweetheart, so we had to do it.'

Gran's things: the bunks under the window, the lace curtains, the saucepans and bucket, the rag rug on the floor, Gran's chair, the table and shelves. Then – I can't live in the wagon, thought Kizzy.

'And 'tisn't as if the wagon was any good; it's fallin' to pieces – no use to anyone, darlin'.'

'It was to me.' There was no use now in saying that.

'Never you mind,' Mrs Smith's voice cut across her. 'You'll go to a nice house; nice clothes you'll have and good schooling. You'll end up like a lady,' and Mrs Smith put on her coaxing gypsy voice. 'Wouldn't be surprised,' said Mrs Smith, 'if you won a prize,' but Kizzy was not listening. Panic had set in. 'What will happen to Joe?' asked Kizzy.

She asked that again, made herself ask it, when the flames had died down to smouldering red and they were once again having tea, sitting round their own fire. 'But it's wunnerful warm everywhere,' said Mrs Smith. Only Kizzy was cold; even close to the fire she was shivering. Somewhere a clock struck two, it might have been the House stable clock or the village church clock or one in the next village, everything was so quiet. 'Told you nobody'd be out,' said Mr Smith.

Now that the funeral was over, the wagon burnt, there was a feeling of merriment with the warm fire, tea, and a bottle of rum Lumas Doe had brought out. Kizzy had gone down the orchard, past the wagon's smouldering heap with its smell of burning. She found Joe, who was not grazing, but standing, hanging his head; when she put her arms round him his neck was wet with sweat, as she was wet under her clothes, and now, round the fire, with the laughing and talking, she had to ask her question. 'What'll happen to Joe?'

'Who's Joe?'

That was Mr Smith. 'He wouldn't know,' Uncle Jess said it with fresh scorn. 'Me own grandson and doesn't know a hoss from a chair leg. Joe's the Lovells' old hoss.'

'What'll happen to him?' Kizzy had risen and stood shaking by the fire.

'We'll find him a home,' said Lumas Doe.

'A *good* one?' asked Kizzy. Her lips would not keep still.

Lumas Doe was feeling jovial. 'Oh *dordy*, a very, very good one. The best for old hosses.'

'He . . . won't be worked too hard?'

'He'll have plenty of rest,' and Lumas and Mr

Smith started laughing, but when at last the fire grew low and they went to the trailer, caravan and tents, and Kizzy was in the tent with Boyo, Boyo said, 'I know what they'll do with your Joe.'

Boyo had a camp bed and was muffled in a quilt; Kizzy was in a corner on the ground; she had not known how thin the straw of her mattress was nor how threadbare her blankets – in the wagon they had seemed perfectly warm; now she lay freezing though she was in all her clothes, her knees drawn up under the cardigan. 'Do you know what they'll do with your Joe?'

'No,' said Kizzy.

Boyo's big face peered at her from the bed. 'Sell him to the knackers.'

'What's the knackers?'

'Horse meat. They'll sell him for the hounds.'

'F-for what?' quavered Kizzy. She had risen in her bed.

'To eat, silly. He'll be torn up,' said Boyo. 'Those dogs will tear him up and eat him.' Then Kizzy did to Boyo Doe's face what she had done to Prue Cuthbert's stomach, drove her fist right into it.

Boyo let out a howl and Mrs Doe darted from her caravan. 'She hit me, Mam, she hit me,' sobbed Boyo while Kizzy stood silent and sullen. Mrs Doe was already upset from the argument with Uncle Jess, the burning of the wagon, and an uneasy feeling about Kizzy herself; she took it out in temper. 'That's

27

enough of you,' she said to Kizzy, boxed her ears and gave her a hard slap in the face.

For Kizzy too it was enough. Gran had lammed her back and bottom but no one had ever slapped her face; the smart of it, the tingling in her ears seemed to make a glare in front of her eyes, the pain ran down into her throat and choked her. She gave a hard dry sob, turned on Mrs Doe and bit her through the hand.

Mrs Doe shook her off as if she were a small dog and hurled her back on her mattress. 'Us, take in that diddakoi,' Kizzy heard her shouting to Mrs Smith. 'Savage, that's what she is.'

'Give her a taste of the cosh,' Mrs Smith shouted back but Mrs Doe had slammed the caravan door.

Kizzy lay in a little heap in the corner of the tent; her ears were still singing, her cheek smarted, but that was nothing to the pain in her heart. Joe. Give Joe to the knackers, to the hounds . . . She felt sick, yet, at the same time, black with hate against Boyo who taunted, Mrs Doe who hit, Lumas Doe who lied. She thought of going to Uncle Jess but he was fast asleep in the Smiths' trailer. There was no one but herself, she, Kizzy, and as the night drew out, she knew what it was she had to do.

Boyo was asleep, snuffling on his camp bed. Cautiously Kizzy got up, pulled on her boots and stole out of the tent. Both the trailer and caravan were shut up because of the bitter cold and there was no sound as she stole between them. All that was left of the wagon was a big heap of smouldering ashes with a red-hot centre and she crouched there a little while, warming herself; as the hardness went out of her body, Kizzy found she was making whimpering noises like a little animal. They were small noises but Joe heard them, though he was across the orchard, and quietly he came up and stood behind her, snorting softly as he smelled the fire. Alarmed that someone might hear him, Kizzy got to her feet. 'We mustn't stay here,' she whispered. For a moment she hugged Joe, then went to the apple tree where his halter was hung. 'C'mon,' she whispered and obediently he bent down his head. She slipped the halter on and, taking the rope, she led him, keeping well away from the trailer, caravan and tents, round the edge of the orchard to the gap in the hedge; it was barred by a plank which she cautiously slid out. She led Joe through on to the road, keeping him on the verge so that his heavy hooves made no sound.

The road was black, high hedges made it darker and cut off the stars, but travellers need no torch, their eyes seem to see in the dark and Kizzy could guide herself and Joe. When they came to a gate, she stopped him beside it, climbed the bars and scrambled on to his back. Then, still holding the rope and kicking him gently to send him along, without a sound they rode away into the night.

★

Admiral Twiss was having breakfast. It was said in the village that he ate off a newspaper spread on the table and that he and Peters and Nat lived off whisky, hard-boiled eggs, food out of tins, 'and everything fried.' 'Very bad for them,' said Mrs Cuthbert. 'But do you wonder − no woman to do anything. They say the house is dreadfully neglected.' The village could only 'say' because it did not know; Mrs Cuthbert, or any other of the village women, were never invited in, not even into the hall. The Vicar could have told them, or Mr Fraser, the school's headmaster, or Doctor Harwell; they often dined at the House and played chess or bridge with Admiral Twiss, but they were quiet men and did not talk. The villagers were sorry for the Admiral. 'I don't know how they manage,' Mrs Cuthbert told Miss Brooke.

'They all look well-groomed and well-fed,' Miss Brooke pointed out and indeed that morning the Admiral had an old-fashioned breakfast: coffee, porridge − he liked it with salt − kidneys on toast served in a silver dish, more toast and marmalade. It was true that Admiral Twiss looked a little lonely − the cloth was laid at one end of the long mahogany table that could seat twenty people − but the table-cloth was fresh, 'every morning,' said Peters; the delicate patterned china shone with cleanliness as did the silver, the whole room. 'Women chase dirt,' said Peters. 'I deal with it.' Indeed he always seemed to have a vacuum cleaner in his hand. Twice a year, when the Admiral went away – in spring for the racing at Aintree, the Topham Trophy and Grand National, in August to the Dublin Horse Show – a London firm, 'of men,' said Peters, came down and gave the House a thorough cleaning from attics to cellars; the rest of the time most of the rooms were closed. The groundsman who looked after the cricket pitches cut the lawns and clipped the hedges; there were no flowerbeds, only a tangled jungle where flowers had been, but Peters kept the vegetable garden with an old man who came from the village every day. The 'old 'un', as they called him, looked after the greenhouses too. 'It's not impeccable but it's all in order,' said Admiral Twiss, 'and peaceful,' he might have added.

Peters usually served the Admiral in the companionable silence they kept together, but this morning he seemed excited – excited for Peters, which meant his eyes were even bluer than their usual speedwell blue, his forehead was flushed and he limped more quickly. Something had happened, but Peters did not speak of it until the Admiral had finished, nor did the Admiral ask him, but when he wiped his moustaches and put the napkin down, 'Admiral Sir,' said Peters, 'the little girl is here.'

'What little girl?'

'From the orchard. You know they burned the wagon last night.'

'Yes, the old woman wanted it,' said Admiral Twiss.

'Well, that's their business,' said Peters. 'Nat just went out to quiet the horses – smelled it in the stables they did – but this morning when I come down, there was Mrs Lovell's old horse on the drive.'

'Frightened off?'

'No, sir – it was on a rope and when I opened the front door, the child was asleep on the step – like a frozen bird,' said Peters.

'Good Lord!' said the Admiral.

'Yes, sir. The step and her clothes were covered with snow but the rope was still in her hand, the horse standing there patient, dejected like.'

'How long had they been there?'

'Hours I guess,' said Peters. 'Most like she didn't dare to knock or ring.'

'Why didn't you call me?'

'Hadn't had your breakfast, sir.' In Peters' opinion no small gypsy or, indeed, anyone should interfere with the Admiral's breakfast and, 'I attended to her, sir,' said Peters with dignity.

'What did you do?'

'Called Nat, made over the horse to him. He rubbed it down and gave it gruel with beer. Not used to being in, so he thought best to put it in the yard with some hay. Nice old hoss,' said Peters. 'Nat says it must have been a good 'un once . . . not bony like a gypsy's horse, well-fed.'

'And the child?' asked the Admiral.

'Took her in the kitchen by the fire,' said Peters.

'Got off her boots and clothes, shabby and old but clean – except the boots. Wrapped her up in that old camel hair dressing gown of yours, sir, thought it would be soft and warm; blankets over that with a hot bottle to her feet and stomach. She whimpered from the pain as she warmed. Didn't cry, but her eyes . . .' Peters swallowed. 'Big as teacups they looked in her dirty little face, dirt and tears, sir. I gave her hot milk with an egg beaten up and plenty of sugar, sugar for the shock. There's been a shock, sir.'

'She's seen her home go up in flames.'

'Seems more than that,' said Peters. 'She kept calling, "Joe, where's Joe?" Told her he was safe with Nat and told Nat to keep a sharp eye on him. As she comes round, she keeps begging, "Please can I see Sir Admiral?" That's what she calls you. "Please, please, Sir Admiral".'

'Bring her to the library,' said Admiral Twiss.

'Sir Admiral?'

His dressing gown trailed on the floor behind Kizzy though she tried to hold it up; her bare toes curled away from the feeling of the carpet – she had never been in a room that had a pile carpet before, or long curtains, velvet curtains, and walls made of books, or so it seemed to Kizzy; she could not see them properly because the books seemed to swim round the room, the fire to blaze up and sink down again in an odd way. Kizzy could feel sweat under her

33

curls, her cheeks were hot yet she was shivering. The Admiral was sitting in a chair quite close to her but she found it difficult to say what she had to say; at last she managed to get it out: 'Pl-please, Sir Admiral, d-don't let them take Joe.'

'Let who take him?' The Admiral's voice was quiet.

'The D-Does and S-Smiths.' Kizzy was shaking now. 'They came because of Gran . . .'

The Admiral nodded. 'I fetched them,' and, looking at her, he asked, 'Was that wrong?'

It was a queer question for a gentleman to ask a little gypsy girl, but the Admiral was serious. Kizzy shook her head. 'Someone had to come – for Gran – but Joe . . . Sir Admiral, c-could you k-keep him here with yours? You like horses, Gran said you did. Joe's old, not like yours but sir, he's Joe. Gran said she had had him more'n twenty-five years and now . . .' Kizzy gave a sob, 'they'll send him to the knackers . . . Boyo says he'll be torn up . . . hounds will eat him up . . . Boyo told me and Mrs Doe . . .' Kizzy clenched her fists.

'And what did you do then?' The Admiral was watching her.

'Hit 'em and bit 'em,' said Kizzy. There was a sudden twinkle in the Admiral's eyes but when he spoke he was still serious.

'You didn't tell them you were coming to me?'

Kizzy did not think that worth answering. 'They don't know you,' she said disdainfully.

34

'But you do.'

'I know your Christmas church,' said Kizzy, 'and the little people singing inside.' The Admiral did not ask, 'What little people?' 'And I seen you looking at the hosses.' She lifted her eyes to the Admiral's face and did not even see the bristling eyebrows and moustaches, only his brown eyes that did not look fierce now but kind which, oddly enough, made her want to cry. 'G–Gran knew you,' she said. 'When – when you talked to her, it was d–different.' A tear slid down. 'You l–lifted your hat,' whispered Kizzy.

'Of course,' said the Admiral.

'So I thought you wouldn't let them send Joe to the knackers,' Kizzy said it in a rush as she felt more tears coming.

'Certainly not,' said Admiral Twiss. 'That's no way to treat a fine old horse,' and he took Kizzy's hot small hand into his own cool one. Looking down at it she could see his heavy ring with a bird carved into it on a shield, and the way his veins stood out like cords. She felt too how firm it was. A tear fell on it and the clasp tightened. 'They won't get Joe,' said the Admiral. 'I'll go down and see Lumas Doe,' but there was no need. At that moment they heard a voice arguing. Lumas was standing on the drive, shouting at Peters. The Admiral felt how Kizzy trembled when she heard his voice and, 'Wait here,' he said and, 'Call the man into the hall,' he told Peters.

'Should talk to him on the drive, Admiral Sir. He's

a dirty one,' said Peters, but the Admiral shook his head.

'Well, Lumas,' he said. 'Still taking what isn't yours?' The Admiral's voice was pleasant but, He knows Mr Doe, thought Kizzy, listening.

'Us guessed she was here.' Lumas was belligerent. 'Little varmint! Sneakin' off.'

'Why shouldn't she? It's her horse.'

'Hers?' shouted Lumas.

'Yes.'

'Kids don't own hosses.'

'This one does. Old Mrs Lovell's possessions will go to her next of kin. That's the child, Lumas, not you.'

'What about my expenses?' said Lumas in the ingratiating whine every traveller can adopt. 'Payin' for the funeral an' all.'

'Mrs Lovell paid for her own funeral,' the Admiral said crisply. 'I happen to know because she left the money with me and I paid it to Uncle Jess Smith.'

'But we come over at once,' pleaded Lumas. 'Us and the Smiths. Up sticks and come. That costs something with petrol and all.'

'Not the thirty pounds you would have got from the knackers. You were doing the child out of that. Well, let's say you had a certain amount of trouble and you did the job well, so I shall give you twenty pounds. Take it and keep clear of the horse.'

'Twenty!' Lumas was outraged.

'Twenty.'

'Make it twenty-five.' Lumas tried to make his whine more ingratiating.

'Twenty and you're lucky.' Her eye to the door, Kizzy saw Admiral Twiss take out his wallet. At the sight of the notes and the sound of their paper crackle, Lumas's whole face changed, as Kizzy had known it would.

He put out his hand, then stopped. A gleam had come into his eye. Unlike Mr Smith, Lumas Doe liked horses – young ones he would have said. 'You wouldn' trade with that roan colt, sir?'

'I would not,' and the Admiral said to Peters, 'Get his receipt, then give him the money.'

Admiral Twiss came back to Kizzy. 'That is settled,' he said. 'We'll put Joe in the small meadow. It has buttercups in summer and he'll be under Nat's eye. No one can get him there.'

'Sir Admir . . .' but Kizzy did not finish saying it. The book-lined walls that had seemed to swim, the fire that blazed up and down, blurred together in front of her eyes; she tottered in the camel hair dressing gown. 'I . . . don't feel . . . very w-well,' gasped Kizzy.

'Pneumonia,' said Doctor Harwell. 'Strange. I have never known a gypsy child get it before.'

'She's been through bad distress,' said Admiral Twiss.

'And up all night,' said Peters.

'I'll call the ambulance.' Doctor Harwell shut his case. 'Though I don't like moving her in this weather.'

'It's not only that.' The Admiral said it slowly. 'For a traveller child to go into hospital is harder than for most. They're not used to central heating, bright lights, modern clatter. She . . .' and Admiral Twiss took the plunge, 'she had better stay here.'

'You would have to get a nurse.'

The Admiral and Peters exchanged glances of consternation. 'But she would be a woman,' said Peters.

'Naturally.' Doctor Harwell could not help smiling at their faces.

'We needn't have a nurse,' said the Admiral. 'If you will give us your instructions, I can get Mrs Doe or Mrs Smith up to see to her,' but when Doctor Harwell had left and Admiral Twiss walked down to the orchard, it was empty; the Does and Smiths had gone. 'Taken your twenty pounds and moved out,' said Peters. All that was left were droppings of Joe's, the small ash of the fire and a bigger pile, still smoking, of the wagon with, lying in it, the bent and blackened iron hoops of the wheels. 'In any case, they wouldn't stay on a site where there had been a death,' said the Admiral, but the Does and Smiths had not kept the orchard rules: tins and rubbish lay about and, 'I can guess we shan't see them again,' said Admiral Twiss.

Chapter Three

In Mrs Blount's classroom Kizzy's place stayed empty. 'I suppose those other travellers have taken her away,' said Mrs Blount.

'That is what I'm afraid has happened.' Mr Blount was discouraged. 'It's not much use trying with those children. They're here today and gone tomorrow,' but it seemed Kizzy was not gone. Soon the wildest rumours were in the school and village: the wicked travellers had set the Lovell caravan on fire, stolen everything in it: Admiral Twiss had chased the travellers out of the orchard and burned the wagon himself. Then, Kizzy Lovell was at the House with Admiral Twiss. The boys and girls looked at one another. With Admiral Twiss! 'Impossible,' said the village, but it was not impossible. Mrs Cuthbert had it from the butcher's boy – he had delivered beef for making beef tea. Kizzy was ill. She had been burnt in the fire. Nat had been seen in Rye buying things at the chemist: a child's hot-water bottle: cough syrup: prescriptions. Kizzy had not been burnt. She had pneumonia.

'Pneumonia!' Mrs Blount felt guilty. 'I knew she had no coat,' she told Miss Brooke. 'I knew and did nothing about it.'

'Dear Mildred, that wouldn't have given her pneumonia,' said Miss Brooke.

For a while Kizzy did not know where she was, at Amberhurst House or anywhere else; she was too ill. There were days of pain and struggling for breath; Peters sponged her burning forehead and wrists with cool water, gave her sips of water or ice cream, but to her he was only a face that loomed near and went away. There were nights when she cried out or screamed in terror about Joe and the knacker . . . the wagon and flames . . . Boyo . . . Mrs Doe's slap . . . and about school. The Admiral, who sat up with her, learned a great deal about school in those nights. 'Diddakoi,' cried Kizzy. 'Gypsy gypsy joker, get a red hot poker . . . When's your birthday? . . . bump bump . . . Don't pull my hair – don't, don't!' It rose to a shriek and the Admiral had to quiet her. He, Peters and Nat took it in turns to stay with Kizzy and it was amazing how gentle and thorough were those male hands that lifted her, changed her, tended her, but Kizzy did not know anything about it until she woke one morning when outside the sun was shining from a sky as blue as the quilt that covered her, and she found herself in a small room, sparsely furnished as old-fashioned rooms for children often were, a little shabby but with a fire burning that sent firelight up the walls. The wallpaper had a pattern of apple blossom, faded now so that it was only a suggestion but, in her haziness, it made Kizzy feel she was back in the orchard. Yet when she looked at herself, was it herself? Were these her own hands and arms and, as she looked under the bedclothes, her own legs? She was wearing a striped jacket and trousers and, I'm clean, thought Kizzy. She had a moment of panic, then Nat was there with his comforting horse smell. "S'all right, you're at the House,' said Nat.

'Joe?' croaked Kizzy.

'Safe and well and waiting for the buttercups. Now drink this,' said Nat.

'Who is going to look after her?' asked Mrs Blount.

'They are,' said Miss Brooke.

'Those three men!'

'But how can they?' and that was what the village asked. 'How can they? Poor mite, in that great house,' and, 'Men can't look after a sick child.' Mrs Cuthbert said it positively, but the Admiral, Peters and Nat looked after Kizzy so well that Doctor Harwell had to agree she did not need a nurse. It was Peters who washed her and gave her a blanket bath every day, washing her with warm water and soap as gently as any woman, an arm or leg at a time, the rest folded in warm blankets; it was Peters who sent Nat into Rye to buy bath powder, a brush and comb and pyjamas. Nat bought boys' pyjamas – he would not go into a woman's or girl's shop, but as Kizzy had never had any she did not know the difference. 'I slept in my vest,' she told Nat. Peters made her meals, bringing her soup or milk and honey in little cups, or a spoonful or two of jelly and, when her throat was sore, ice cream.

Kizzy was far too thin; 'Underweight,' said Doctor Harwell, 'and under-nourished.'

'Well, I can guess they lived on bread and tea.' Admiral Twiss was vexed with himself. 'Mrs Lovell had probably grown too old to cook.'

'It seems the child wouldn't eat the school dinners. Her teacher thinks the other children told her that hers weren't paid for.'

'Not only that,' said Mr Blount, who had come up to the House about Kizzy. 'She tore her meat with her fingers and that shocked them.'

'I ought to have thought about food,' said the Admiral. 'I knew the child was there, but one scarcely ever saw her.'

Now Peters was building Kizzy up – in every way. 'Drink this up, saucepot.' 'Now I don't want a crumb left of that.' He kept her room clean and polished, with a fire that burned day and night; when it was dusk Kizzy lay and watched the firelight flickering on the walls and ceiling. The fire made work; Peters had to carry coals up twice a day, 'but an electric fire dries the air,' said Peters. 'Not good for her lungs.'

When he was busy, Nat came and sat with her. He

rubbed her back – 'Coo! your bones stick out like a chicken's,' said Nat – and told her stories of the horses he had looked after: of Royal who had run in the Derby and the Admiral's favourite show hunter, Rainbird. 'Best of all classes at Richmond. I'll show you his cups and some of the rosettes when you are well,' but even Nat's stories were not as good as the Admiral's, especially the one about Joe. He told Kizzy how Joe had been foaled – 'Must be twenty-eight years ago. He's one of the oldest horses I have ever seen,' – foaled on a farm in Antrim, 'which is in Ireland.' How he had been trained as a hunter, lunged over fences and, as a five-year-old, been taken to Dublin for the Summer Show. How he had been bought and travelled on the ferry to England, and of the cups and rosettes he, like Rainbird, had won. How, one day, Joe had put his foot in a rabbit hole and broken a bone in his fetlock, 'so he couldn't jump any more.' Then how Kizzy's grandfather had bought Joe in a sale and Joe had pulled the wagon along the country lanes in England, following the strawberry, hops and apple picking from Kent to Worcestershire and back again, but always landing up in the Admiral's orchard to spend the winter, until at last he had stayed there all the time with Gran. It was a made-up story, of course, 'But it might have been Joe?' asked Kizzy. 'It easily might,' said the Admiral.

Every morning he would wrap her in the camel hair dressing gown and carry her to the window and

Nat brought Joe, in his halter, on to the drive below. Then the Admiral would put Kizzy in a small rocking chair – she was allowed to sit up now – tuck a rug round her and Peters would bring their 'elevenses' on a silver tray, a mug of milk for Kizzy, coffee for the Admiral, and they would have them together. These days of convalescence were perhaps the happiest Kizzy had ever known. With Gran she had been content, but now she was radiantly happy until she had – 'visitors' said Kizzy.

'I am Kizzy Lovell's teacher. May I see her, please?' It was Peters' afternoon out and when the bell rang, Admiral Twiss answered the door. 'You would never have been let in, else,' said Mrs Cuthbert.

'It isn't curiosity,' Mrs Blount told the Admiral quickly and, 'What could I do but let her in,' he told Peters afterwards.

'Kizzy,' said the Admiral when he had opened the bedroom door. 'Your teacher has come to see you,' but where was Kizzy? At the word 'teacher' she had dived to the bottom of the bed under the bedclothes. 'School doesn't seem to be popular,' said the Admiral.

Mrs Blount was distressed. 'I tried, indeed I did, but some of them teased her, children can be cruel. Perhaps if I had done what Miss Brooke said . . .'

'What did she say?'

'Try to make them interested in her, make her

44

romantic . . . I thought it was rather nonsense at the time.'

'Sounds more like sense,' and the Admiral asked, 'Is that the Miss Brooke who has just been made a magistrate?'

'I never know how to place Olivia Brooke,' Mrs Cuthbert had had to admit. It was annoying as, usually, given half an hour, she had people clearly and properly labelled, 'as if we were all tidy glass jars,' said Miss Brooke.

'Glass jars? I never said that.' Mrs Cuthbert was nettled. 'And what do *you* think people are?'

'More like caves to explore,' said Miss Brooke. 'Mysterious caves. One never gets to the end of them.'

'Well, if anyone's mysterious, Olivia, you are.'

Miss Brooke had bought the cottage and appeared in the village without any explanation; the village liked things explained, but Miss Brooke had seemed to be so busy making her new garden that she had little time to talk and, though Olivia, as they soon called her, was perfectly friendly, for all her probings Mrs Cuthbert had learned little more.

Miss Brooke was small and, 'When you really look at her,' said Mrs Cuthbert, 'very plain,' with a pale face and mouse hair twisted into a bun, but her hazel eyes were remarkable and deceived one into thinking her pretty, which was odd as she did not seem to bother much about clothes and never went to a hairdresser.

Mrs Cuthbert knew too that she had strange habits – Mildred Blount had told her how the supper things were often left unwashed because Miss Brooke wanted to listen to music, nor would she answer the door while it was going on. 'Sometimes she doesn't do a thing in the house but make her bed,' Mrs Blount reported. 'She goes straight out to garden.'

'If it's a fine day, why not?' Miss Brooke asked, unperturbed.

'She doesn't seem to care a fig what people think,' said Mrs Blount, 'and yet she's not proud. You couldn't call her that.'

'N-no,' said Mrs Cuthbert.

Mr Blount was a staunch admirer. 'Look how she took Mildred and me in while we were waiting for our house. Kindness itself.'

'Ye-es,' said Mrs Cuthbert. The truth was that Miss Brooke had a poise for which Mrs Cuthbert could see no reason; she was obviously poor – the cottage was simple almost to bareness, 'And she makes her own bread.'

'I like making it,' said Miss Brooke. She would bake and garden but would not sew or knit or join the flower-arranging classes for which Mrs Cuthbert was recruiting. 'But you're so fond of flowers, Olivia.'

'In my garden, or in cottage bunches,' said Miss Brooke.

She would take the most menial tasks at village gatherings, seeming to prefer washing-up behind the scenes to figuring on committees or meeting people – 'Even when the Princess came to open the Hospital wing,' said Mrs Blount – so that it was a shock to the village when Miss Brooke was made a Justice of the Peace. 'They must know something about her we don't,' said Mrs Blount.

'Still, I don't understand it,' said Mrs Cuthbert, who would dearly have liked to be a magistrate herself. 'She's so mousy and quiet.'

'Perhaps it's because she is quiet.' That was the Vicar. 'She listens and doesn't interrupt.'

'And lets you get a word in,' said Doctor Harwell, who had wanted her on the Hospital Board. In fact, Miss Brooke could have been on several committees but, unlike Mrs Cuthbert, did not want to be. 'The Court work is enough if I do it properly,' said Miss Brooke, 'and I like my house and garden.'

'If you ask me, she'd rather talk to flowers than humans,' said Mrs Cuthbert. The Admiral would have understood that; he would rather have talked to horses and, 'She seems a wise person,' he said now.

Mrs Blount blushed – it was almost as if he had called her unwise – and she turned to the little mound hidden far down in the bed. 'Kizzy, come out,' she coaxed. 'I have something for you. Something she ought to have had long ago,' she told the Admiral. 'It might have prevented this. I blame myself.'

Admiral Twiss stripped off the bedclothes, took Kizzy and sat her upright against her pillows. 'Sit up at once,' he said sternly. 'Give your hand to your teacher and say "How do you do". We don't behave like this at Amberhurst.'

Kizzy reluctantly held out her hand; Mrs Blount took it and, watching the Admiral's eyebrows, did not keep it but shook it politely and laid it down; then she put a big paper bag on the bed, a fresh bag with the name of a shop on it. 'It's a warm coat for you,' she told Kizzy. 'For you. It hasn't belonged to anyone else. It's new. Won't you open it?'

'Open it.' The Admiral's order was curt, as he might have spoken to a rating on the bridge of his flagship.

It was a duffel coat, new as Mrs Blount said, of soft, thick brown wool, with a hood and a plaid lining in scarlet and blue and polished wood toggles for buttons.

'I can guess that you bought that with your own money,' said the Admiral and Mrs Blount nodded.

'I felt guilty.'

'You shouldn't have.' The eyebrows and moustaches worked. 'I believe you have just married, Mrs Blount, and are getting a new house.'

'Yes,' she blushed again. 'We hope to move in next week.'

'So you must need every penny, every moment. Very good of you to do this,' said Admiral Twiss.

Mrs Blount had hoped Kizzy might smile, give a gasp of surprise and pleasure, but Kizzy did not open her lips; nor, when she had lifted the coat out of the bag, did she touch it again. 'See, it still has the tickets on it.' As Mrs Blount spread the coat on the bed, she sounded as if she were pleading.

'Say "thank you",' said the Admiral to Kizzy.

'Thank you,' emotionless.

'You can wear it when you come back to school,' Mrs Blount said. Kizzy went still as a stone and, when Admiral Twiss had taken Mrs Blount away and Kizzy, listening, had heard her footsteps growing fainter down the drive, she took the duffel coat and threw it out of the window.

Peters found it on the drive and brought it in to the Admiral, who did not lam Kizzy as Gran had lammed her when she put Prue's clothes down the apple tree. He told Peters to dry the coat, brush it and hang it up. 'She'll wear it by and by.'

'Will I have to go back to school?' Kizzy asked the Admiral.

'Of course. When you are well.'

'I am still ill,' said Kizzy.

'You are much better.'

'I'm not.'

'Don't you want to get up?'

Kizzy thought. 'Tell you what,' she said. 'I'll stay in bed till four o'clock, then get up and have my breakfast. When I go to bed at night I'll stay there until four o'clock next day.'

As if the coat had sparked it off, 'She can get up and

dress now,' said Doctor Harwell – but Kizzy could not, she had nothing to dress in. Peters had burnt her clothes – 'That's all they were fit for,' – and thrown away her old boots. 'Leakin',' he said. 'I'm afraid we'll have to buy her some clothes, Admiral Sir.'

'You or Nat had better go into Rye.'

There was a silence, then: 'Wouldn't be much good in girls' shops, Nat and I.' Peters was decided. 'And think of the gossip,' – and for once the gnomes rebelled. 'I know, sir,' said Peters. 'If you went up to London you could get everything she needs in one big shop and no one the wiser. Much better for Kizzy, sir,' but Admiral Twiss, who had fought his way through with convoys to Russia in the war, been torpedoed twice and won the Distinguished Service Order, quailed. 'Just jerseys and skirts, sir,' Peters tried to encourage him. 'Those pinafore things . . . I'll measure her for you,' said Peters helpfully, but the Admiral was still appalled. 'Peters,' he whispered, 'What . . . what do they wear underneath?'

Peters made a chart in which a paper-doll Kizzy had her measurements laid out like a diagram for a ship, height, width, depth, and Admiral Twiss went to London and walked along Oxford Street looking at the shop windows, but there were so many filled with small girls' clothes that he was bewildered. He knew where to get his shoes made, buy his hats, order his shirts, but this . . . At last he went to his tailor and ordered a jacket he did not need. Then, 'Phipps,' he said, 'what's the best place to buy children's clothes?'

'Rowe's of Bond Street,' said Phipps.

That was quite close, but when he found it the Admiral stood looking at the window for a long time: a model girl was wearing a pale blue coat with a velvet collar and white gloves; another had a yellow silk smock; they did not at all look like Kizzy. There was, too, a little girl figure in riding clothes; Admiral Twiss admired the cut of the jodhpurs, the fitted tweed jacket showing a glimpse of white shirt and brown tie, the brown velvet riding hat. Must get Kiz a pony, he thought, then suddenly recollected she was not his. He looked at the blue coat again, shook his head and went away.

He took refuge at his barber's and had a haircut though his hair did not really need one. 'John,' he asked the young barber. 'You have children?'

'Three, sir.'

'Where do you buy their clothes?'

'Marks and Sparks, sir. Marks and Spencers, that is – branches all over the place. Wonderful value they are. One of their biggest shops is in Oxford Street.'

It was a big shop. Admiral Twiss wandered up and down its aisles where the goods were set out on long counters or hung on rails. The shop was full and after Amberhurst seemed to the Admiral a nightmare of movement and noise; he was jostled and hustled, the lights dazzled him. He did find a rack full of children's dressing gowns and it occurred to him that Kizzy ought to have a dressing gown of her own, that his was too large for her, but he could see no one to serve him. The Admiral was used to small exclusive shops where assistants, full of deference, sprang to meet him; he did not understand that he should search for what he needed and then find a salesgirl – added to which he did not really know what he should buy. After a little while he gave up, hailed a taxi, and went to his Club for lunch. 'Luncheon and a stiff drink,' said the Admiral. Then he caught the next train home.

'Well, well,' said Peters. 'Probably have been the same meself. No use sending Nat. We'll have to ask that Mrs Blount.'

'And have trouble with Kizzy? Besides, Mrs Blount would surely talk.'

'It would be all over the village,' and, 'If we want *that*,' said Peters, 'better to ask Mrs Cuthbert.'

The Admiral was pondering. 'There's one woman who doesn't talk,' he said. 'I will go and ask Miss Brooke.'

'Two of everything?' Miss Brooke asked in a business-like way. 'Or three?'

'But is three enough? I buy shirts and socks in dozens,' said Admiral Twiss.

'This is a child. They grow,' and Miss Brooke said, 'One on, one off and one in the wash. That's enough.'

'But you will get her – er – everything?' asked the Admiral.

'Of course. Pyjamas, vests, pants, tights. That's what they wear these days. I had better get them in London if you don't want talk. I'll go up tomorrow, won't bring them but have them sent express. I will make out a list and keep an account.'

'Handkerchiefs,' said the Admiral suddenly. 'She ought to have those – I like mine of lawn, hand-rolled.'

'I will find her some pretty ones.'

'A hat? Shouldn't she have a hat? And an umbrella?'

'I can guess Kizzy wouldn't know what to do with them.' Then, 'My dear Admiral,' said Miss Brooke, as he handed her ten ten-pound notes, 'I shan't need all that. Thirty pounds should do it but I will take forty in case; it's no use buying too cheaply.' She peeled off four notes and gave him back the rest. 'Thank you, Admiral.'

'Thank *you*.' It was heartfelt and, as he turned from the cottage, 'That's done,' said Admiral Twiss, relieved. Somehow it never crossed his mind not to trust Miss Brooke.

The clothes arrived in boxes from London and were so pretty Kizzy forgot they brought school nearer. There were three sets of underclothes, pink, blue, white, scattered with flowers: two skirts, one plaid, one cherry red, as if Miss Brooke knew she liked bright colours; there were jerseys, a warm cardigan, a pair of walking shoes and a red pair to wear in the house – Kizzy had never had shoes before, only boots. She was puzzled by the handkerchiefs. 'Thought they were for wearing round her neck,' Peters told the Admiral. 'Only they're too small,' said Kizzy. 'What are they for?' and, when Peters told her, 'Blow your nose on a *handkerchief!*' Kizzy was shocked. 'I have a finger and thumb, haven't I?' she wanted to say. 'Or else my skirt.'

She went in to the Admiral: 'Thank you for choosing my clothes.'

'I didn't choose them.'

Kizzy's head jerked up. 'Who did?'

'Miss Brooke. A nice lady.'

Kizzy scowled. 'I don't like nice ladies.'

When she was dressed and looked at herself in a long mirror, she only recognized herself by her curls and the gold rings in her ears. She had grown taller and thinner – and paler, thought Kizzy, or was that because she was washed? Gran had washed her each night before she went to bed, carrying the water in a bucket, but here it was not only every day, 'Three times a day,' said Kizzy – and at night in a bathtub. She sniffed her hands; they smelled freshly of soap and a longing swept over her for the old smell of wood smoke, of open air and Joe. 'When can we go back?' Kizzy could have cried. It was then she had her second visitor.

★

The Easter holidays had started and, 'I'm going to the House,' Clem Oliver told his mother.

'Do you think you should?' Mrs Oliver was doubtful.

'I'm a boy . . . Admiral Twiss won't mind and that little girl's my friend,' and, sure enough, Kizzy broke into one of her rare smiles when Peters brought Clem up. 'Clem! You've come to see *me*!' She was dazzled.

'Sure,' said Clem, and, 'What a house!' he said. '*What* a house!'

'Is it?' asked Kizzy. She did not know enough about houses to judge. 'It's nice and old.'

She meant that Amberhurst House, in spite of its grandeur, was comfortably shabby. 'Well, generations of us have lived here,' Admiral Twiss would have said but, 'I wouldn't like to,' said Clem. Coming from his bustling crowded farmhouse home, Amberhurst seemed huge and empty to Clem. Admiral Twiss, he thought, must be lonely. The kitchens where Clem had come in and this nursery wing above it were smaller, warmer, more homely but, 'Think of coming down that great stone staircase for breakfast,' said Clem, 'and having it at that long table with the big silver candlesticks – one little place at the end.' Clem had seen it when Peters took him in to the Admiral. 'And libraries and drawing rooms, a billiard room, a gunroom. His bedroom must have empty rooms all round it – and all them portraits staring down at you.

No, thank you,' said Clem, yet Amberhurst was friendly to him.

He had tea in the kitchen with Kizzy, Nat and Peters. 'Mr Peters made us sausages and chips and he made scones. He can cook as well as you, Mum,' Clem told his mother. Admiral Twiss was not there; he dined alone at eight, but after tea he showed Clem his racing cups, his fishing-rods – he promised to let Clem fish the lake and trout stream – and the workshop where he made his models. 'Cor! it was fascinating,' Clem told at home. 'He's making a tug, it'll work with real steam. You should see it.'

Kizzy was pleased – and flattered – by Clem's visit. 'He's one of the biggest boys in the school, but he came to see *me*,' she boasted to Peters.

'Nice lad,' said Peters. Nat said the same and the Admiral said Clem could come when he liked, but Kizzy's time of peace at Amberhurst House was over. The world outside was beginning to creep in.

'Clem Oliver went up to Amberhurst.'

'He had tea at the House.'

'Went to see the little gypsy.'

'Clem Oliver.'

'If Clem went, why not me?' said Prudence Cuthbert.

'Kizzy can go out,' Doctor Harwell put away his stethoscope. 'She's over it well. You made an excellent job of her,' he said to Peters. 'She can go out but wrap her up well.'

'You can come with me this morning to see Joe,' the Admiral told her.

'In his meadow?' Kizzy's face was lit with joy.

'Yes, but put on your coat.'

The joy departed. 'Haven't got a coat,' muttered Kizzy.

'Yes, you have,' said Admiral Twiss. 'The coat Mrs Blount gave you. It's hanging in the cloakroom.'

'*That* coat!'

'That coat,' said Admiral Twiss and added, 'No coat and you don't come and see Joe.' He walked away down the drive. Slowly Kizzy went to the cloakroom to get the coat.

'You see, Kiz,' said the Admiral when they had seen Joe – he had put her up on his back, she had hugged the huge old neck and they had given Joe apples – 'We can't always do as we like.'

'That's only children,' Kizzy burst out.

'It isn't only children, unfortunately,' the Admiral sounded sad, 'and it isn't only the coat.' He had buttoned Kizzy into it, put up the hood. 'The coat isn't all we shall have to accept, you and I.'

'I want to see Kizzy Lovell.'

Though Peters did not like women he was not, normally, cross to little girls, but something in Prudence's sharp little face, her primped-up hair, bright pink coat and smart white shoes, made him feel dislike; dislike, too, for the imperious way she spoke which was quite different from Clem's 'Please, sir, could I see Kizzy?' 'I want to see Kizzy Lovell,' said Prue.

'But does she want to see you?' Peters' barrel shape filled the back door.

'But I have come to see her.' Prudence was surprised.

'We don't have to see everyone who comes. You wait there, young lady, while I go and ask.' But it was not easy to keep Prudence Cuthbert out, as Miss Brooke or Mrs Blount could have told him. Prue slipped into the kitchen after Peters and came face to face with Kizzy.

Kizzy had stood rooted by the kitchen table as soon as she heard Prue's voice. Prue stopped too when she saw her and they looked at one another, 'like two kittens with their fur on end,' Peters told the Admiral afterwards. Then, 'Go away,' said Kizzy.

'That's nice,' said Prue. 'When I have come all this way to see you.' Kizzy knew that was not true. Prudence had come to see Amberhurst House. 'So she could tell about it at school,' said Kizzy afterwards.

'Clem went, so why can't I?' Prudence had told the girls.

'You'd never dare.'

'I would.'

'They won't let you in.'

'We'll see,' and Prudence had tossed her head. Now she was in, though only as far as the kitchen and, 'Go away,' said Kizzy.

Prue had sleeked her fur down. 'You'll be coming back to school soon, so I thought we could be friends,' but Kizzy knew Prue did not really mean it; she was too busy looking over Kizzy's shoulder down the corridor where a baize door led into the House. 'Couldn't we?' coaxed Prudence, looking longingly at the door.

'No,' said Kizzy.

'You have nice clothes,' said Prudence admiringly. 'You look really pretty.'

'Go away.'

Prudence's fur rose up again. 'You needn't be so high and mighty just because you're up at the House. Soon as you're well you'll have to leave, my Mum said so. They're having a meeting about you next week. Probably they'll put you in a Home. How'll you like that?'

'I won't live in a Home,' said Kizzy.

'Where'll you live then?' taunted Prue.

'I shall live by myself.'

'Don't be soft. Anyway, your caravan's burnt.'

Kizzy's chin came up. 'Sir Admiral's going to make me a little wagon, just for my own.'

'I don't believe you.'

'He is.'

'I don't believe it.'

59

'He is. He is!' Admiral Twiss heard that child's cry in his study. 'He is!' and he got up.

'Then he's barmy.' The Admiral was in time to see Prudence and Kizzy fly at one another, kicking and spitting and biting in fury until Peters took each of them by the back of the neck and shook them apart.

Mrs Cuthbert came up to complain and met the Admiral on the drive. 'An absolute little savage,' she shrilled. 'Prudence came home black and blue with a huge scratch on her cheek.'

'You should see the scratch on Kizzy's,' said the Admiral.

Peters was more severe. 'That's no way to behave,' he told Kizzy. 'Even however horrid she is.'

'I'll always do it to anyone horrid,' declared Kizzy.

'None of your lip, saucepot; while you're at Amberhurst you'll behave. If you *come* from Amberhurst you'll behave, or you'll disgrace us at the meeting.'

Kizzy stared at him. So it was true: there was to be a meeting. She felt suddenly cold.

Admiral Twiss was in his workshop putting the last touches on the miniature tug, the *Elsie May*, when Kizzy appeared. She watched, her head almost level with the high workshop table, as his long clever fingers fitted a cage of brass over the little starboard light. 'Just in case she collides with anything,' he explained, and said, 'When I tried her out on the lake one of the swans attacked her. Can't protect the searchlight though; it must swivel as she changes direction.' No one but the Admiral, thought Kizzy, could make a tiny searchlight that swivelled. She took a deep breath.

'Will you make a wagon for me?'

The Admiral gave her a shrewd glance from under his eyebrows, then said, 'I only make models.'

'Will you – buy me a wagon?'

'When you are eighteen.' His fingers did not falter as he worked over the light and, without any unnecessary questions, he added, 'They wouldn't let you live in one until you are eighteen. Then they couldn't stop you.'

'Can't I live with you?'

He shook his head. 'They wouldn't let us, Kiz.'

'Why not?'

'We haven't a woman here.'

'Why do you need a woman when you have me? I looked after Gran.'

'I know you did.'

'I could sell bunches of flowers, and pegs if you would make them for me; that could pay for me if you haven't enough money.'

The Admiral stopped fitting the cage, took Kizzy's hand and led her into the library; he sat down in his chair and drew her to stand against his knee. 'At this meeting, Kiz, they will decide that Amberhurst

House isn't a fit place for a little girl and we cannot argue.'

Kizzy did argue.

'A little girl lived here once, Clem says so.'

'This is a girl's room,' Clem had said, looking round Kizzy's bedroom.

'Is it?' Again Kizzy had not enough experience of rooms to know.

'Yes, look at it.' And certainly the white bed, the miniature dressing table, the small white rocking chair, blue carpet, muslin curtains and apple blossom paper looked like a girl's. 'I thought they only had boys,' Clem had said, 'but there must have been a girl.'

'Long long ago,' Admiral Twiss said now and added, 'There's a painting of her in the drawing room.'

They went together into the big disused drawing room with its pale green panelled walls and stiff brocade curtains; the chairs and sofas had dust sheets over them but Kizzy could see small gilded tables, faint colours of embroidered carpets, a mirror framed in gold. Over the fireplace was a life-size painting of a little girl, much the same age as Kizzy but with a thin, fine-boned face that was like the Admiral's; she had his brown eyes too and they seemed to follow Kizzy across the room. The girl had brown ringlets and was wearing a dress of maroon cloth with full white muslin sleeves, and a wide band of blue velvet running round the skirt. 'You can tell it's velvet though it's only painted,' whispered Kizzy in awe. The small bodice was laced in blue up to a narrow white ruffle at the neck; the hands were holding a spray of roses. 'I can guess she would rather they had been a pair of reins,' said the Admiral. 'She grew up to be a fine horsewoman.'

'Who was she?' asked Kizzy.

'My grandmother.'

'Your *Gran* . . . but she's a little girl.'

'Girls grow up,' said the Admiral. 'She married my grandfather – married very young. Her name was Kezia Cunningham; she was the last Cunningham. My grandfather was another Admiral Twiss, but because Amberhurst House and the land were hers, they called themselves Cunningham Twiss.'

'Like you,' said Kizzy.

'Like me. They had sons, the eldest was my father. My father had me – my mother died soon after I was born – so you see there were only boys.' Kizzy studied the painting. Though she did not like girls, she liked this one; the brown eyes were steady and friendly.

'Kezia Cunningham Twiss – did she sleep in my room?' Kizzy asked.

'It was hers when she was a child. Come to think of it, Kiz, you might have been called after her. Kizzy might be from Kezia. She knew your Gran; they were friends. She liked gypsies.'

Kizzy looked at her again. 'Kezia.' It gave her a curiously happy feeling to think they shared a name. 'When was her birthday?' Kizzy asked it earnestly.

'I must look it up,' and back in the library Admiral Twiss opened a big Bible that had a stand all to itself. 'Here we are: Kezia Cunningham, born December 9th, 1858.'

'I'll take it for mine,' and, just as she had studied the painting, Kizzy pored over the writing, the list of names.

'All our family are in this book,' said the Admiral.

'Wish I could be in it,' said Kizzy and sighed. 'She would have wanted me to stay, especially if I'm Kezia.'

The Admiral did not answer.

'No one comes to the house,' argued Kizzy, ''cept Clem and he wouldn't let on. Suppose you told everyone that I had gone away, Mrs Doe had taken me, and I stayed here in your grandmother's room until I was eighteen?'

The Admiral ran his hand through Kizzy's curls. 'They wouldn't let us, Kiz.'

'They wouldn't know, only you and Peters and Nat, and they wouldn't tell either. I could stay here with you and them – and Joe – and I wouldn't have to go to school.'

'It's a nice idea,' said Admiral Twiss, 'but it wouldn't do.'

Kizzy set her lips.

Chapter Four

'The case of Kizzy Lovell'.

The Children's Department had decided to bring it before the Court, 'Because we're flummoxed,' said Mr Blount.

The main room of a Town Hall, even of such a small town as Rye, seemed an oddly impressive place in which to discuss the fate of a small diddakoi.

The stairs up to it were wide with a heavy red cord on brass links as a banister rail. In the vestibule was a wooden model of a ship under a great glass dome that caught the light. The room itself was high, wide and long, with high windows. There was a dais at one end, a big table below; it took anyone walking from the door a good many steps to reach that table, especially if they were child steps.

Above the dais were the royal arms of England, the lion and the unicorn in gold and blue; below them a shield with the arms of Rye, three lions rampant on three ships' sterns in gold. All round the walls were panels lettered in gold with the names of the reigning king and queen, all the kings and queens of England from the time of Edward the First, 1272, and of all the mayors of Rye who had served in their reigns. From the ceiling hung heavy gilded chandeliers.

Now the table was covered with papers, a group of people sat along three sides with the Chairman's higher-backed chair in the centre; he had a woman magistrate on either side, the one on the left was Miss Brooke. Mr Blount as the Children's Officer was there, and Doctor Harwell; so, also, to their annoyance, was Mrs Cuthbert. 'Of course I should be there,' Mrs Cuthbert had said. 'Wasn't I the one who discovered Kizzy? And I am on the School Board.' She had been determined and indignant.

Mr Blount had written Kizzy's story as briefly as possible; he also had a letter about her from the Admiral. 'Please read them to the Court,' said the Chairman and, when they were finished, 'Go on, Mr Blount.'

'Well, sir, Admiral Sir Archibald Cunningham Twiss kept Kizzy while she was ill—'

Mr Blount was interrupted by Mrs Cuthbert: 'She ought to have gone to hospital. I said so at the time.'

'. . . while she was ill,' repeated Mr Blount, 'but she is well now and, for all the Admiral's kindness, we doubt if it's fit, sir, for her to stay on at Amberhurst House.'

'Not with three old men,' said Mrs Cuthbert and Doctor Harwell was nettled to reply, after he had looked at the Chairman for permission, 'I believe

66

Admiral Twiss is sixty, Peters, the houseman, in his fifties, while Nat might be forty-five,' said Doctor Harwell. 'That is not old.'

'Too old to look after a child.'

'Please don't speak out of order, Mrs Cuthbert,' and the Chairman resumed, 'It seems they looked after her very well. We have Doctor Harwell's report, but even if it were desirable, it would not be fair to ask Admiral Twiss to—'

'Keep her.' Mrs Cuthbert could not resist finishing for him. 'Of course not. She must go into a Home.'

Ignoring Mrs Cuthbert, the Chairman asked Mr Blount, 'You have tried all your register of foster-parents?'

'Yes sir, but it isn't easy to place a traveller child.' Mr Blount looked worried. 'They seem . . . afraid of her, sir.'

'Well, do you wonder,' Mrs Cuthbert broke in again. 'She's a little wildcat. There was trouble at school and you should see the scratching she gave my Prue. She's dirty—'

'Not now,' said Mr Blount.

'Not even house-trained.'

'She is now.'

'And they say she hasn't a vestige of table manners.'

'Mr Blount! Mrs Cuthbert! May I remind you we are in Court where we do *not* speak out of order.'

'I'm sorry, sir.' Mr Blount was ruffled but Mrs Cuthbert closed her bag with an angry snap as, 'Miss

Brooke,' the Chairman turned to her. 'I think you have something to say?'

'Only that you can't expect to have table manners when you haven't a table. Some gypsy children eat with their fingers and wipe them on their hair afterwards.'

'Ugh!' said Mrs Cuthbert.

'It isn't "ugh" to them. They believe it makes hair soft and silky – and you know, in some ways they think us dirty.'

'Us? *Dirty?*' Mrs Cuthbert was incredulous.

'More than dirty,' said Miss Brooke. 'A gypsy might refuse to have a cup of tea with you because he can't be sure of how you wash your china.'

'*Well!*' Mrs Cuthbert almost spluttered.

'You might use the same bowl for washing out clothes,' said Miss Brooke. 'They use separate ones. You might put your tea towels in the spin dryer with your bed-linen or underclothes. I think we must remember –' Miss Brooke said to the Board and flushed as if she did not like laying down the law, ' – try to remember – we are dealing with different standards and different doesn't mean bad.'

'A wise reminder,' said the Chairman. 'I think, Mr Blount, you should bring in the child.'

Mr Blount fetched Kizzy, who was waiting in the vestibule with Peters; she came in, her shoes shined as carefully as the Admiral's, her coat brushed, her hair brushed too, glossy with cleanliness, 'and a look on her face like the devil himself,' said Peters, who, when he had handed her over, went and stared out of the window, rubbing his eyes with the back of his hand. 'Fool that I am,' said Peters.

Mr Blount led Kizzy over that long floor to the table. 'Gracious!' said Mrs Cuthbert. 'I hadn't realized how small she is, almost undersized.'

'Not,' said Kizzy through her teeth.

'Mrs Cuthbert, once again, will you kindly keep quiet?' and the Chairman leaned forward to Kizzy. 'Kizzy, you know some of us, Doctor Harwell, Mr Blount — and Mrs Cuthbert.' At that name, the black look grew blacker. 'But we are all here to try and help you.'

No response, only a glower from under the curls.

'Now will you tell us, Kizzy, if there is anyone anywhere with whom you would like to live?'

The reply was blunt. 'What's the use my tellin' when you won't let me?'

'How do you know? Let's try.' The Chairman was encouraging. 'Isn't there anyone?'

'Meself.' An involuntary smile went round. Kizzy saw it and scowled.

'Yourself? But, Kizzy, little girls of seven — I believe you are seven — can't live quite by themselves.'

'See?' said Kizzy with scorn. 'I knew that's what you'd say.' She became aware that Mr Blount was holding her hand and, 'Let *go* of me,' she screamed violently to Mr Blount, wrenching her hand away.

'Lemme *go*.' The child shriek rose to the windows as Kizzy tried for the door, but the Usher was blocking the way and Mr Blount caught her. Kizzy was brought back to the table, her breath coming in gasps. Leaning on the sill in the corridor, Peters put his hands over his ears and shut his eyes.

'All right, Mr Blount.' The Chairman waved Mr Blount away. 'Now Kizzy, stand still and look at me.'

'Look at the gentleman when he tells you!'

'*Mrs Cuthbert!*' The Chairman's voice was sharp, and he ordered, 'No one is to speak to the child except us, the magistrates.' Then he turned to Kizzy and said gently, 'Mr Blount will not hold you, no one will touch you if you talk to us properly, so let's be sensible,' and Kizzy stood quietly though she held the edge of the table and her breath still came in gasps. 'Now listen to me, Kizzy,' said the Chairman. 'I'm afraid we can't allow you to live by yourself and, though I'm sure Admiral Twiss will always be your friend, we can't let you stay at Amberhurst House – for several reasons. This means we must find another home for you, doesn't it?'

No answer but the glowering, the small gasps.

'Doesn't it?'

Still no answer.

'You try,' the Chairman said to the woman magistrate on his right who, in her turn, leaned forward. 'Kizzy.'

Kizzy had obediently looked at the Chairman – in

any other circumstances she would have liked him – but she was wary of ladies and though she had realized there were two others in the room besides Mrs Cuthbert, a large lady and a small one, had kept her eyes away from them. Now it was the large one who was speaking in a soft coaxing voice: 'Kizzy, wouldn't you like to go where there are other girls and boys?'

No answer but an increased glowering, deeper gasps.

'You would have someone to play with,' coaxed the magistrate, 'as if you had brothers and sisters. Wouldn't it be nice, Kizzy, to have a sister?'

It was unfortunate she said 'sister'. A look of desperation came into Kizzy's eyes – as if she were trapped, thought Miss Brooke. Then Kizzy spat. The spit landed plop on the table and there was a silence as all of them stared at the little wet insult and Kizzy ran, this time succeeding in dodging the Usher. Peters caught her outside the door.

'Well!' The kind magistrate was nonplussed, as were they all – the Court was not used to defiance from a seven-year-old. 'Oh dear, I'm afraid I precipitated that.'

'What did I tell you?' said Mrs Cuthbert in triumph and, when the Usher had wiped up the blob of spittle, the Chairman said, half laughingly, half sadly, 'Gypsies undoubtedly should stay with gypsies.'

'They usually do,' said Mr Blount. 'This is the first

case concerning one of their children that has ever come my way.' He paused. 'As you see, it's difficult.'

'I like her spirit,' said the Chairman. 'But . . .'

'It's pitiful,' said the magistrate.

'Precisely.' The Chairman was brisk – magistrates must not be emotional. 'Now, to get back to business: the question is, what can we do with her? We could make a Care Order, Mr Blount, handing her over to your authority's care, in which case you would have to find somewhere for her to live. Any other suggestions? Yes, Doctor Harwell?'

'There's always St Agatha's,' but Doctor Harwell said it hesitantly. 'They would never refuse . . .' There was a silence.

'St Agatha's is an excellent Home,' said the Chairman, 'but it is big. There have to be rules . . . What do you think, Mr Blount?'

'I believe she would have a hard time there . . .'

'So would the nuns,' said Mrs Cuthbert.

'If we could find something more individual, sir.' Mr Blount cast what he hoped was a quelling look at Mrs Cuthbert. 'As you have seen, Kizzy doesn't take to the suggestion of other children. I expect she finds them strange – as they find her. She has made friends with a boy, Clem Oliver, but he's the only one.'

'Admiral Twiss says in his letter she has always been solitary,' said the Chairman. 'Perhaps if you could find a childless couple . . .'

Mr Blount shook his head. 'No one seems willing, sir.'

There was another silence; then Miss Brooke turned to the Chairman, who said, 'You have an idea, Miss Brooke?'

'I know fostering should, properly, be done by a family,' said Miss Brooke, 'a man and wife so that the child can have, as it were, a father and mother, but Kizzy has never known either, so perhaps she is different . . . and she isn't a baby, but already seven, as far as we can tell. Now that the Blounts have moved into a house of their own,' Miss Brooke smiled at Mr Blount, 'I have an empty room. I could take Kizzy.'

'You?' They all stared.

'Yes.'

'After *that* exhibition?' Mrs Cuthbert was incredulous.

'Particularly after that.' There was a flush on Miss Brooke's cheeks again. 'I have always been interested in gypsies and have, oddly enough, several times been drawn into having to do with them. I was a magistrate for a good many years in our home county of Berkshire . . .'

Mrs Cuthbert sat up.

'We had two gypsy cases – children not going to school. When I was a barrister—'

'You were a barrister, Miss Brooke?'

'Yes,' and Miss Brooke anticipated Mrs Cuthbert by saying, 'I retired to look after my father. Once on circuit I defended a gypsy family. I think I understand what it means to be homeless, and a little of how to deal with driven people; one of my father's stable lads, too, was a gypsy.'

'You kept stables then?' As Miss Brooke went back into her past, Mrs Cuthbert grew more and more agog. 'You must have had a big house.'

'We befriended him,' Miss Brooke went on as if Mrs Cuthbert had not spoken. 'He taught me something about his people and gave me a little personal experience. With Kizzy it might not be a success, but I could try, though I'm afraid my cottage will seem rather narrow to her.'

'A cottage has far more space than a caravan,' said the Chairman.

'Yes, but her wagon was open – she lived outside – and Amberhurst House, where she has been since, is so spacious. However, my cottage is the last in the village, on the edge of the common; Kizzy might not feel shut in.'

'And I am not far away,' Mrs Cuthbert chimed in. 'I can help.'

'I will only do it on condition that I am not helped.' Miss Brooke's flush had deepened but her words were firm. 'Except by Mr Blount, of course. Yes, it will be difficult. I think we all realize now that for a time Kizzy will be unhappy, perhaps hostile . . .'

'Hostile! How dare . . .' Mrs Cuthbert was breaking in again, but the Chairman raised a peremptory hand. '*Madam!* I will not have you interrupting; if you persist, I will order you to leave the Court.' Then, 'Miss Brooke,' he said, 'you really are prepared to take this – hostile – child?'

'What would we be in her place?' Miss Brooke said it simply. 'Yes, I would be prepared to do it – prepared to try.'

'Mr Blount?' The Chairman turned to the Officer, but Mrs Cuthbert broke in again, though a subdued Mrs Cuthbert. 'May I say something, sir?'

'At least she asked,' the Chairman said to Miss Brooke afterwards, 'although she didn't wait for the permission!'

'Forgive me for being personal, Olivia,' said Mrs Cuthbert, 'but it's my duty to ask – especially,' she said to the Chairman, 'as Miss Brooke refuses help. Though she may have had experience on committees, should a single woman take a child into her home?'

'Thank you, Mrs Cuthbert, but Miss Brooke isn't, if I may say so, the usual single woman; nor is this a usual child – in fact, so unusual that we should be grateful for any solution, let alone such a promising one – but *may* we hear,' he said with another stern look at Mrs Cuthbert, 'what Mr Blount thinks?'

'That it's an excellent idea,' said Mr Blount, and the Court ruled that Kizzy would go to live with Miss Brooke, 'and be supervised, from time to time,' said the Chairman, 'by Mr Blount.' It was settled – began to be settled, Kizzy would have said.

★

Term had begun and, 'This is the morning,' said Admiral Twiss. He had sent for Kizzy after breakfast. 'Peters is taking you to school. Then he will pack up your things and take them to Miss Brooke. She will fetch you.'

Miss Brooke had not spoken while Kizzy was in the courtroom so that Kizzy had hardly noticed her, but she had since come to Amberhurst House, 'to meet Kizzy properly.' 'Told you so,' said Peters. 'Once one of 'em comes, others will follow. Told you so.'

If Peters was frozen, he was nothing to Kizzy. Admiral Twiss had introduced her in the library and Kizzy had not spoken – 'Not once,' he told Peters – Miss Brooke had not tried to make her; after she had said, 'Good afternoon, Kizzy,' she had talked to the Admiral.

At first it was stilted – Admiral Twiss was almost furiously shy – then she asked him about his silver cups and he showed them to her. 'These were Rainbird's.' 'These were Royal's,' and soon he was talking of horse shows and racing as easily as if she had been Nat, 'until she brought me up short,' the Admiral told Nat afterwards. 'Yes, that was a good day,' he had said of a certain race meeting. 'I remember China Court won the Great Metropolitan Stakes—'

'Not China Court – Mirzador,' said Miss Brooke and, as the Admiral stared at her, 'I know because my father trained him.'

76

'Your *father*? Then . . . your father . . .'

'Was Gerald Brooke.'

'Good Gad!' and the Admiral turned to Kizzy. 'Miss Brooke's father was a famous racehorse trainer, so you see she must like horses too.'

Kizzy only scowled.

As Miss Brooke sat in the big chair opposite him where, since his grandmother, the Admiral could not remember any woman sitting, he wondered how it was that she had come to live at Amberhurst. He vaguely remembered hearing that when Gerald Brooke died he had left scarcely any money, but Miss Brooke told no more about herself; she talked of the horses, of Amberhurst, of Kizzy, but he found himself looking rather than listening and, when she got up to go, had an effort to stop himself from saying, 'You know, you smile with your eyes.' There could be no pretence in a smile like that and he had felt heartened for Kizzy.

Now he got up from the breakfast table and blew his nose on his handkerchief; his eyebrows were working as he took Kizzy to the library and sat down by the fire and, as he had always done, drew her to him, but she stood, stiff and as unwilling as a block of wood. 'It's no good, Kiz,' said the Admiral. 'We have to go through with this, but I want you to know that you will always be my girl, and Peters' and Nat's, and I want to make a bargain with you.'

'What?' whispered Kizzy. She was looking at his

ring with the bird on the shield, remembering the first time she had seen it; now too, her eyes were hot with tears.

'I will promise to look after Joe for you and you'll come up every Saturday and spend the day with us; Miss Brooke says you can – Sunday as well if you like – but *you* must promise to do everything Miss Brooke tells you.'

'And if I don't?' The words seemed to drop from Kizzy's lips.

'They may say we have taught you bad ways and won't let you see us, which would be sad for us both. I should give your promise, Kiz. Promise you'll do what Miss Brooke says.'

'I promise.'

'Gypsy's promise,' said the Admiral. 'Gypsies keep their word.'

Kizzy nodded – but gypsies have a way of wriggling round it, as the Admiral ought to have known.

Miss Brooke drove to the school to fetch Kizzy, but when Mrs Blount went to look for her, 'Kizzy's gone,' she said, astonished. 'I told her to wait for you.'

'Which is probably why she has gone.'

'Do you think she has run back to the House? Poor you, having to chase after her,' but Miss Brooke did not have to chase. She drove slowly along the lanes and there at the gates was Kizzy, standing in the road, an uncertain lost little figure. When Miss Brooke stopped the car, Kizzy turned a small mutinous back, but there was something she learned at once about Miss Brooke; like the Admiral, she did not ask questions. 'Where do you think you are going? Why didn't you wait for me as you were told?' Instead, 'Kizzy, it's time for tea,' said Miss Brooke. 'I can drive behind you, if you like, but if I were you I should get in.'

'I won't eat your food or drink your drink and I won't talk to you,' said Kizzy at the table.

'That won't be very interesting for either of us, will it?' Miss Brooke answered in a calm voice.

The table was drawn up to the window where there were hyacinths in pots. Miss Brooke had made cheese toasts, they were in a hot dish; the home-made currant buns had a spicy fragrant smell; there was home-made raspberry jam and the tea was hot in the brown teapot, but Kizzy took from her pocket one of the two crusts she had saved from school dinner and put it on her plate. It was so dry she could hardly bite it, but she did not touch the butter or jam. Miss Brooke did not seem upset but went on eating and drinking and, when Kizzy had finished, calmly cleared away. Kizzy heard her humming as she washed up. She doesn't care, thought Kizzy, and her heart sank. There did not seem anything for her to do so she sat down on the hearthrug and stroked Miss Brooke's tabby cat. She liked the cat.

'His name is Chuff,' Miss Brooke called from the kitchen. Kizzy withdrew her hand.

Presently Miss Brooke came in; she did not, as most of her neighbours did, turn on the television and take out her knitting or sewing, but sat down, picked up a book and, careful not to glance at Kizzy, began to read aloud.

'*Once upon a time*,' read Miss Brooke, '*there was a prince who hadn't much money, but he had a kingdom, and though this was quite small, it was large enough to marry on, and marry he would . . .*'

Out of the corner of her eye, Miss Brooke could see Kizzy's attention was caught, perhaps because she was surprised – no one had ever read to her, just by herself, before. '*Still it was rather bold of him to say straight out to the Emperor's daughter, "Will you have me?" but sure enough she did . . .*' Miss Brooke's voice was enchanting and, as she read, the cottage room seemed to be filled with the story of the swineherd, the prince disguised, the proud princess, the tittuping ladies-in-waiting, the emperor in his old slippers. Kizzy on the hearthrug was still and Miss Brooke put more expression into her voice; it was some time before she saw that Kizzy had her hands over her ears.

In the wagon Kizzy had gone to bed when Gran went, but in people's houses children, it seemed, had bedtimes; at the House, Peters had bundled Kizzy off at seven o'clock; she would have liked to know if it was the same here but, as she had announced she would not talk to Miss Brooke, she could not ask. Then, as the clock in the tiny hall struck seven, 'Time for bed,' said Miss Brooke.

When she had shown Kizzy her room it had been meant as a surprise; the room was little, high up in the roof so that the ceiling sloped; when the window was open at night, it seemed to be up in the stars, and in it was Kezia Cunningham's furniture from Amberhurst House: the white bed, small dressing table and rocker, the blue carpet. 'Admiral Twiss thought they would make you feel more at home.' Miss Brooke did not mention the fact that she had painted the walls and bought the bedside lamp, papered the wardrobe inside and hung up Kizzy's clothes, put her linen away in a white chest of drawers. 'And here's a shelf for your things.' What things? Kizzy might have asked, but she said nothing.

If Miss Brooke were disappointed, she had not shown it and now she took Kizzy upstairs.

'Needs a woman to look after her!' Peters had chuckled. 'Wait till she tries to give Kiz a bath.'

'Does she object?' asked the Admiral.

'Like a mad cat,' said Peters.

'What did you do?'

'Held her down with one hand and scrubbed her with the other,' said Peters, 'but they'll try and coax and wheedle; they always do.'

Miss Brooke did not coax or wheedle. 'Here is the

bathroom,' she said, 'and your pyjamas and dressing gown. You may not like having a bath, but you can stand in the tub and give yourself a wash with this,' and she showed Kizzy a hand-shower. Miss Brooke had counted on Kizzy's being fascinated by the shower and she was right. A gleam came in Kizzy's eyes and she was betrayed into speaking. "S'like a little watering can,' she said.

'Well, you can water yourself – but be careful, it's hot.' Miss Brooke showed her how to regulate the taps. 'Don't water the walls.'

It was a pity she said that because it was exactly what Kizzy intended, but she had promised to do, or not do, everything Miss Brooke said. She watered the floor instead.

Water flooded the bathroom and began to flow on to the landing and down the stairs. Kizzy turned off the shower and waited until Miss Brooke came up. 'You didn't tell me not to,' said Kizzy. She was standing in her pyjamas on an island of bath mat and towels and ducked her head for Miss Brooke to lam her, but again Miss Brooke did not; for a moment her hazel eyes flashed as if she were angry, then, 'You have had pneumonia,' she said, 'so I can't ask you to help me mop it up.' She picked Kizzy off the towels and felt her. 'Your feet are like ice. I'll get you a hot bottle.'

She put Kizzy into bed and in a few minutes a bottle wrapped in a shawl was at her feet; Miss Brooke brushed her hair, being careful not to pull as

Peters did, then said, 'When you are sleepy, put out the light. Would you like a book?'

Kizzy shook her head. Soon she was deliciously warm but through the open door she could see Miss Brooke's head with its smooth silky hair bent down, her back bent too as she knelt mopping, her hands red now from wringing water out of the cloths. Miss Brooke looked tired. Kizzy remembered Miss Brooke had fetched her from school or, rather, the House gates, and not said a word of reproach; she thought of the cheese toasts and raspberry jam, the story by the fire. She looked round the pretty room made ready for her, her clothes hung up, the ones for tomorrow folded carefully on her chair; she felt the hot bottle at her feet and the gentle way Miss Brooke had spoken – even after the water.

Peters would have chuckled but not the Admiral. 'What would Sir Admiral think of you?' an uneasy voice in Kizzy seemed to ask and she saw, not his eyes, but little Kezia Cunningham's from the portrait in Amberhurst drawing room. Perhaps because Kizzy had her furniture, Kezia's eyes seemed to be looking at her and, '*She* wouldn't have done anything mean,' said the voice. Kizzy almost got out of bed and went to help with the mopping; she would have with Gran though Gran surely would have lammed her. Kizzy almost got up – almost, not quite.

Since Gran had died – no, since she, Kizzy, went to school – a feeling had grown in her that she had not felt before, a resentment that made her stiff and hard, angry against everyone except the Admiral, Peters, Nat, and Clem. 'Everyone! I hate 'em,' Kizzy would have said. Most of all she had to hate Miss Brooke, but it was proving difficult. 'It mustn't be difficult,' Kizzy whispered to herself through clenched teeth and burrowed into the pillow to shut out the sight of her. Then she pricked up her ears.

Someone had opened the front door – without knocking – and Kizzy lay still as she heard Mrs Cuthbert's voice. 'I just popped in, Olivia, to see how you were getting on.'

Kizzy held her breath. Would Miss Brooke tell? This is a private battle, Kizzy wanted to say, but Miss Brooke might . . . Then, 'As well as can be expected, thank you,' said Miss Brooke.

A little later Kizzy heard her coming upstairs. She had put the pail and cloths away and came into Kizzy's room, and again Kizzy held her breath but, 'Goodnight, Kizzy. I hope you are warm now. Sleep well,' and Miss Brooke bent down and kissed her. When she had gone, Kizzy burst into tears.

Miss Brooke had not told Mrs Cuthbert but she did not mind telling the Admiral when he telephoned, even about the tears.

'Did you go in to her?'

'I thought they were good tears,' said Miss Brooke, 'so I let things be.'

'Come to think of it,' said Peters, when the Admiral told him, 'there are very few women who will let things be.'

Surprisingly, Peters had begun to know Miss Brooke, 'a little,' he would have said. When he and Nat had taken the furniture down he had asked her, 'Who will put up the bed?'

'I will, by and by,' said Miss Brooke.

Peters had looked at her small hands and slight body and said, 'We'll do it for you. Don't suppose you're much good with a spanner.'

'You would be surprised,' said Miss Brooke, 'but I should be grateful.' She smiled with her eyes, as the Admiral had noted.

'We'll put the carpet down, if you like,' said Peters gruffly.

'Thank you.'

The carpet did not quite cover the boards and, 'I will stain them,' said Miss Brooke. 'I painted the walls.'

'Didn't make a bad job of it, but floors are men's work. We'll nip into Rye and get a pot of quick dry and do it now. Then it will be done,' said Peters.

He and Nat stained the floor – 'In a woman's house!' said Admiral Twiss – and the woman brought them a tray with mugs of hot coffee and a plate of fresh baked scones. 'Didn't say a word, just put it down,' said Peters; he sounded almost approving. He did not add that as they were going, Miss Brooke smiled at them again; though he did not mention it, Peters remembered that smile.

If gypsies are clever at finding their way round things so was Miss Brooke.

At breakfast next morning, when Kizzy was eating her second crust – Miss Brooke had coffee and scrambled eggs – 'I have asked Clem Oliver to tea,' said Miss Brooke. Kizzy stared at her plate; she knew what Miss Brooke meant; if Clem came, Kizzy could not let him eat alone, she would have to eat her tea. She darted Miss Brooke a look, half hate, half admiration.

Miss Brooke made girdle scones, dropped them hot on the children's plates and poured on golden syrup. 'Supersonic!' said Clem; there was gingerbread and potted ham sandwiches, and Kizzy had to admit to herself it was better even than Peters' teas – admit, too, she was grateful to Clem – because she was really hungry, but, of course, she did not admit it aloud. Clem could not come to tea every day, though, and on the next, the crusts were back.

They had to be back. Kizzy could not put it into words but she knew it would complicate everything if she grew to like Miss Brooke. Then I couldn't be bad to her, thought Kizzy. If only Miss Brooke would command her to eat . . . Admiral Twiss suggested that. 'She promised she would do what you told her. She will keep her promise. You have only to tell her.'

'I know,' Miss Brooke had said. 'But I should rather she did it of her own will. I don't want an obedient child seething like a little cauldron underneath.'

It was Mrs Cuthbert who unwittingly settled it. Saturday and Sunday Kizzy had spent at the House — 'Thank goodness she will eat there,' said Miss Brooke. They were blissful days; to begin with, Miss Brooke produced, not school clothes and the hated coat, but jeans, a jersey, a scarlet anorak and, not shoes, but gumboots. 'If you are to be in the meadow with Joe, you will need them, but remember, take them off when you go into the house.' Kizzy gave a sigh; no one took off boots to go into a wagon.

But the weekend was soon over and it was Monday again — Kizzy produced the crusts. Miss Brooke said nothing but at teatime her face was so sad that Kizzy could not bear to look at her. Miss Brooke helped herself to a hot parsley potato cake and had just begun her tea when there was a knock at the door, Mrs Cuthbert walked in — and instantly saw the crusts.

'Well, *really*, Olivia! Is *that* what you give the poor child?'

'It's what she prefers.' Miss Brooke's voice was level. 'Would you like some tea, Edna?' But Mrs Cuthbert was indignant. 'You let her eat those and sit here gorging yourself?' She was looking at the potato cakes, crisp and brown and parsleyed. 'I shouldn't have thought it of you, Olivia, really I shouldn't,' said Mrs

Cuthbert. 'After all, you take good money for her. It's cheating. Kizzy, you come along to my house and have tea with Prudence and me.'

'Never. Never. Never,' said Kizzy's eyes. Mrs Cuthbert was not to know that in her fierce little heart Kizzy blamed her for everything that had happened: 'If I hadn't gone to school, Gran wouldn't have died.' Kizzy was positive about that. 'Our wagon wouldn't have been burnt. Mr Doe couldn't have tried to send Joe to the knacker. I wouldn't have had pneumonia.' If she had not had pneumonia she would not have made such friends as the Admiral, Peters and Nat, but she was too angry to think of that and, 'I can eat crusts if I like, can't I, Miss Brooke?' she said.

'I don't see why not,' said Miss Brooke.

'She lets me eat anything I like,' boasted Kizzy and, with her eyes glaring at Mrs Cuthbert, she stretched out her hand and took a bun – Miss Brooke had just baked them – and a large helping of jam. 'Jam and buns and crusts,' said Kizzy.

'And potato cakes,' said Miss Brooke, slipping two on to Kizzy's plate. 'You see, things are not so bad, Edna,' Miss Brooke said to Mrs Cuthbert, 'though it's kind of you to ask Kizzy. Say "thank you", Kizzy.'

'Thank you,' said Kizzy, eating.

'Don't speak with your mouth full,' said Mrs Cuthbert.

'Miss Brooke told me to say thank you.'

Mrs Cuthbert snorted and, 'The whole village will

know that I have starved Kizzy,' Miss Brooke said to the Admiral on the telephone that night. 'Never mind, she is eating now,' but the triumph was short-lived. That was Monday; on Tuesday Kizzy ran away.

She ran straight from school to Amberhurst House – and Admiral Twiss sent her straight back to Miss Brooke with Peters. 'But she didn't tell me not to run away,' protested Kizzy.

'You knew that you shouldn't,' said the Admiral.

Kizzy knew it and ran away next day – to the House.

'What's got into you?' asked Peters. 'You used to have some sense. This isn't any good.'

Kizzy was mute and on the next day, Thursday: 'She's here again,' Peters told the Admiral.

Admiral Twiss had to take steps, but took them carefully. 'If you go on like this, Kiz, they will make us forfeit our Saturdays.'

'Forfeit?'

'Not have them,' said the Admiral. 'Nor Sundays,' and was struck by the look of desperation on Kizzy's face.

The village had, of course, seen Peters bringing Kizzy back. 'At least a hundred pairs of eyes,' said Peters.

'So shaming for you,' Mrs Cuthbert condoled with Miss Brooke. 'Have you punished her?'

Miss Brooke shook her head. 'She must have a reason.'

'Reason my foot,' said Mrs Cuthbert. 'You're too soft, Olivia. She simply wants to get her own way. Well, I said it wouldn't do. That child needs a foster-father to discipline her.'

'Are fathers much good at disciplining little girls?'

'Besides, she needs other children.'

'Other children?' Miss Brooke was thoughtful; then, 'I wonder,' said Miss Brooke.

On Friday at five o'clock Miss Brooke telephoned the House. 'Kizzy hasn't come home and it's getting late. Is she with you?'

'She hasn't come,' said Admiral Twiss.

'Where can she be?' Miss Brooke was worried.

'Wait,' said the Admiral suddenly. 'At least, I will ring you back. I have an idea where we might find her.'

He went out and crossed the lawns where the evening light shone on the chestnut trees, and walked through the paddocks till he came to the meadow. There was Joe, swishing his tail in the long grass and, lying curled on his back, what Admiral Twiss expected to see: a small shape in a brown duffel coat.

Kizzy was so cold they were afraid she might get pneumonia again, 'so Peters is warming her and giving her some tea,' the Admiral telephoned. It was he who brought her back to Miss Brooke, 'and stayed two hours,' said Mrs Cuthbert.

'Kizzy, you make me very sad,' he had said as they were driving in the car.

Kizzy was sitting upright, staring with dark eyes at the headlights' beam that, in the dusk, seemed to be sweeping her, a helpless atom, towards the village. 'Not half as sad as I am,' said Kizzy.

'But what *is* it?' asked Admiral Twiss. He was in a chair by Miss Brooke's fire where she had asked him to wait while she gave Kizzy a hot shower and got her to bed. 'But Peters said you would never bath her,' the Admiral said.

'We manage like this,' said Miss Brooke. Admiral Twiss was beginning to think Miss Brooke could manage anything. He found himself at ease and comfortable by her fireside, sipping the whisky she brought him. 'I need a sherry,' she had said. He studied her face as she sat opposite in the firelight – it might be plain but he liked it – good cheekbones and a firm little chin, he thought; her hazel eyes were beautiful, thought the Admiral, and steady, which was lucky for Kizzy. 'What can it be?' he asked again. 'Could you get anything out of her?'

'Nothing. It's partly,' said Miss Brooke, 'because, as I feared, the cottage is too narrow for her, the village too close, and partly . . . I wonder if I am right,' said Miss Brooke.

'Have I forfeited?' It was Saturday, the weekend, but scarcely begun: at six o'clock Kizzy was standing by Miss Brooke's bed.

'Forfeited?' Miss Brooke lifted her head and sleep-filled eyes.

'Not having it,' said Kizzy. 'Not going to the House.' Her anxious small face peered down at Miss Brooke in bed. 'Can I go – or have I forfeited?'

'Of course you can go.'

She dropped Kizzy at the gates, a completely different child from the silent sullen little girl of the week. Miss Brooke watched her running up the drive until the scarlet anorak disappeared among the trees, then drove away, feeling more than ever certain.

On Monday morning, 'Kizzy, I must tell you to come straight here from school,' Miss Brooke avoided saying 'home'. 'Straight here.'

Kizzy stopped eating.

'Would it help,' asked Miss Brooke, 'if I came and fetched you?'

For a moment Kizzy's face lit as if a shutter had been opened, then it closed again. 'I would be a baby,' she said.

'Olivia, that child of yours came streaking through the village as if the hounds were after her.'

'Perhaps they were,' but Miss Brooke did not say it, nor had she commented when Kizzy had arrived, hot and out of breath, at barely ten minutes past three. 'I can run fast,' said Kizzy, when she got her breath.

'Is anything the matter, child?' Mrs Cuthbert was

sharp. 'You should tell us if it is.' But the shutter was down.

'Nuthin' 't all,' said Kizzy.

Next afternoon Miss Brooke waited so long she began to think Kizzy had run to the House again; then she saw her come in at the gate. There was something so weary and hopeless in the way she walked that Miss Brooke ran to the door. 'Kizzy?'

The buttons were off her coat, its hood half torn away; her hair was full of mud and she had a graze on her cheek. 'I was caught,' was all she would say.

'But I warned them at school,' said Admiral Twiss on the telephone when Kizzy was in bed. 'She let it all out when she was ill. I told them and warned them. They said they would watch.'

'In school,' said Miss Brooke. 'But not out of school. That's why she ran to Amberhurst House. The children don't go that way and she knew one of you would bring her safely home later. It's the girls. Clem Oliver would fix the boys. I'm sure it's the girls.'

'But little girls . . .'

'Are far the worst,' said Miss Brooke.

The short cut from the school to the village was along a narrow lane beside what the villagers called the big field but which belonged to Amberhurst Park: there were elm trees along it and a thick hedge of may. The children used the lane to go to and from school and next afternoon at a few minutes to three

Miss Brooke stationed herself in the big field behind the hedge where, from a gap, she could look along the lane towards the school.

She heard the bell; next moment a small figure emerged, running, putting on its coat as it ran towards the lane; hard after came a dozen or more girls. Then Kizzy came down, almost by Miss Brooke on the other side of the hedge. 'Yesterday we sewed up her coat sleeves, so she couldn't get it on,' Elizabeth Oliver was to tell, 'and while she was struggling we could catch her, see. Today Prue and Mary Jo asked to go to the loo and nipped out to fasten a string across the lane, low down where she couldn't see it. Cor! she came down full tilt . . .' and, when Kizzy was down, they pounced.

Looking through the leaves, Miss Brooke saw her up again, her knees bleeding, as she stood in a ring of them. 'Don't go too near, she smells,' 'Doesn't now, Barmy Admiral's bought her new clothes,' 'That's why she's so uppity and high and mighty,' 'Mighty-tighty,' 'Dandy-spandy diddakoi,' 'Where's yer cloes pegs, diddakoi?' 'Oh, we don't sell clothes pegs *nowadays*. We're *far* too grand,' 'Goes ridin' in Rolls-Royces.'

'Let me go home,' said Kizzy through tight lips.

'Go on – we're not stopping you,' but Kizzy had not felt one of them skilfully looping a skipping rope round her ankles and making a slip knot; as she turned they pulled it tight and Kizzy went smack on to the lane path. Once she was down again, 'They were like a pack of little wild dogs,' Miss Brooke told the Admiral, 'Go on, then. Go home. Run, tinker, run.' They pulled her up by the arms. 'We'll make you run.' A tree stood out in the lane, a big elm and, holding Kizzy by the arms, two of the bigger girls ran her into it, 'like a child battering-ram,' said Miss Brooke. There was a gate in the hedge and she started running; she reached the gate as they were ramming Kizzy into the tree for the third time. Miss Brooke did not wait to open the gate but swung herself over the top rail and landed in the lane with a brisk thud; they were making too much noise to hear her.

She walked into their midst, parting them before her and, without saying a word, gave each of the girls holding Kizzy a ringing slap with the flat of her hand across their cheeks; they let Kizzy go, she dropped to the ground and lay still, while they stood, shaking their heads as if the slaps had woken them from a dream. The rest stood as shocked and still as if a bucket of cold water had been poured over them.

In silence they watched while Miss Brooke knelt and gently turned Kizzy over. Kizzy's eyes were shut, her head rolled limply, and a gasp went round. 'They've broken her neck.' Miss Brooke pulled back the hood and examined Kizzy's head; there was blood on her curls and a purple mark beginning to swell on her forehead. When Miss Brooke pulled her eyelids up, they could see the whites of her eyes and two of the girls began to sob. 'Is she . . . dead?' Mary Jo spoke in a shocked whisper.

Miss Brooke stood up. 'I think she is stunned, that's all, but yes, you might have killed her.' She looked them over and counted them: 'Mary Jo. Jennifer. Sally and Susan White: Diana. Anne. Carol and Dawn: Judy. Mary Elizabeth. Elizabeth Oliver – you are Clem's sister and Clem is Kizzy's friend! Pauline. Louise. Prudence Cuthbert. Fourteen against one. You cowards!' said Miss Brooke. 'Bullying little cowards.'

A car came down the lane, a car from the school house and the girls caught their breath. It was Mr Fraser, the headmaster.

Chapter Five

Fourteen pairs of girls' eyes watched Mr Fraser's car drive Kizzy and Miss Brooke away. That evening, at home, everyone of the fourteen felt her heart leap each time the telephone rang or anyone knocked at the door. They had seen Doctor Harwell's car drive to the cottage; later Admiral Twiss came. 'Is she very ill then? Will she die?' They stole in one to the other, gathered in groups – and waited.

'It was Prue and Mary Jo,' whispered Susan, who really was a coward. 'It was Jennifer and Anne. When my Mum finds out I shall tell her it was them . . .'

'It was all of us.' Mary Jo was more honest and the anxious questions went on. 'What will they do?' 'What will Miss Brooke?' 'Mr Fraser?' 'Admiral Twiss?' 'How can we go to school tomorrow?' 'But we'll have to.' 'I feel sick,' said Susan. 'What will they do?'

It began to seem they would do nothing, which made the girls more nervous. 'Wait till my Mum and Dad hear,' Sally had said, but it seemed a miracle was in being: the village did not hear. Then was nobody going to tell? 'Remember the time some money was stolen?' said Prue. 'Mr Fraser sent for the parents.' Wouldn't he send for them now? It seemed not; fathers and mothers were going about their ordinary and everyday affairs. 'Is Kizzy not well then?' asked Mrs Cuthbert.

'I'm keeping her in bed for a day or two,' Miss Brooke said smoothly. Then was Miss Brooke not going to tell?

Oddly enough the silence made Susan feel sicker and even Prudence felt filled with unease. The village naturally talked. 'What has happened to the Lovell child now?'

'She fell out of a tree.'

'No, a tree fell on her.'

'She is being X-rayed.'

X-rayed — the girls did not like the sound of that.

When Kizzy opened her eyes to find that, once more, she was in bed but with her head singing and throbbing, two tears had squeezed themselves out from under her lids; only two.

'Cry, Kiz,' said Miss Brooke. 'It will do you good.'

'Won't cry for . . . them,' quavered Kizzy.

'She has a tough little nut,' said Doctor Harwell. 'Fortunately for her — and for them. She'll be all right. Little brutes. I should like to give them all a good tanning.'

'So would I,' said Miss Brooke. 'It would do them good, but it wouldn't help Kizzy.'

'But these are *nice* children,' Mr Fraser had said in bewilderment. 'Most of them are very nice.'

'Until they gang up,' said Miss Brooke.

'Yes,' Mr Fraser sighed. 'One can't understand but one sees it again and again. They gang up on a particular child – probably he or she is nice too. If one clamps down as Mrs Blount did, it goes underground and it's worse for the victim. How can it be dealt with?'

'I think it's dealt with already,' said Miss Brooke. 'For a moment they thought they had killed Kizzy. They won't forget that, and Kizzy, too, isn't quite innocent. She has hit and bitten and scratched and spat. Besides . . .'

'Besides?'

'It's a children's war. Let the children settle it.'

'But . . . if it happens again.'

'It won't,' said Miss Brooke. Elizabeth Oliver, Clem's sister, had told Clem and Clem had come straight round to the cottage. 'It won't. The boys know.'

'Ah!' said Mr Fraser.

'Why don't you pick on someone your own size?' said Clem. 'Rotten little stinkers. Dirty cowards.' From their side of the playground, the boys yelled, 'Scaredy cats. Have to get fourteen of you afore you tackle one,' and,

'Cowardy-cowardy-custard
Can't eat bread and mustard,' the boys sang.

99

Kizzy's empty place was like a sore mark in the classroom. 'I wish Mr Fraser would send for us and tell us off.' Mary Jo spoke for them all. 'It would be even then.'

'I don't mind,' said Prudence loftily. 'I'm glad. I don't care a pin for Kizzy Lovell.'

'You'll soon care,' said Clem, 'if I catch you after her again.'

Prue started to chalk 'Clem Oliver loves Kizzy Lovell' on the wall, but Clem came and rubbed it out with a look of unutterable disdain. 'Kick her,' said one of the boys.

'I don't kick girls,' said Clem, 'but I can give them barley sugar.' Barley sugar was twisting an arm behind the victim's back. He only gave Prue's arm one twist and let her go. 'That's a taste of what you'll get,' said Clem. Prudence hissed like an angry little cat but Clem simply walked away.

'I'm not coming back to school,' Kizzy would have told Clem if she told anyone, but she knew how to keep secrets, which is by not telling anyone at all. 'I can't go to the orchard,' she said to herself in that time in bed. 'They can't have me at the House so, soon as I'm up, I'll get Joe and Joe and me will go away.' She could not say 'run' away because Joe could only plod. She began gathering scraps of food in a carrier bag Miss Brooke said she could have. She had kept every penny of the pocket money Miss Brooke gave her, 'to buy sweets or any little thing you want,' but Kizzy bought nothing. 'Don't you like sweets?' Kizzy did like the few that had come her way, but buying them meant going to the village shop, 'where they ask questions.'

There was one question she herself asked Miss Brooke as soon as her head was better. 'Can I go to the House on Saturday?'

'I expect so – if you keep quiet.'

'I'm always quiet with Joe.'

'Doctor Harwell thinks you can go back to school on Monday.'

To Miss Brooke's surprise Kizzy only nodded, as if it did not matter, yet she must mind, thought Miss Brooke. It must be an ordeal. She looked across at Kizzy's face which seemed – contented, thought Miss Brooke. How could she be contented, this unfathomable child? But Kizzy was far away, far over the Downs on Joe's back. They would walk along at night – when everyone's in bed and no one will see us – and camp in woods and orchards, build a fire; she would collect sticks and pick up old dung for fuel. Why, Joe himself could supply a fire. An old saucepan, thought Kizzy – there was an old one Miss Brooke used for the chickens; she had two so could spare one. I must take matches, planned Kizzy – she had not a flint like Gran's. A blanket, some sacks, a net of hay for Joe – Nat would not miss one – her bag of scraps. I can pick onions and potatoes from people's gardens –

she was small enough to get through hedges – p'raps find an egg. Then, when they were far enough away, she would build a house of branches, or find a hollow tree – 's good I *am* so small – only first she must be well enough at the weekend to go to Amberhurst House.

She would spend Saturday there, get full of food, stuff myself, thought Kizzy, so it will last, collect and hide all her things. Go again on Sunday and, after lunch, when the Admiral and Peters dozed and Nat went to the Lodge to read the Sunday papers, say goodbye to Kezia Cunningham then put the things on Joe, an' we'll just go, thought Kizzy. She suddenly gave Miss Brooke a beaming smile.

'Kizzy,' said Miss Brooke at breakfast. 'Admiral Twiss telephoned last night.'

Kizzy stopped, a piece of toast halfway to her mouth. 'He didn't say I couldn't come? But I must,' she said. 'I have to see Joe.'

Miss Brooke made a queer sound like a hiccough and put down her cup. It seemed as if she were going to say something but changed her mind. 'As soon as you're ready, we'll go.' Kizzy was too busy with her own plans, hiding the blanket, filling her pockets with matches, bringing out the loaded carrier bag, 'scraps for Joe,' she said, which was partly true – there were one or two apples. Miss Brooke made another of her queer noises and, queerly too, did not put Kizzy down at the gates but drove her up to the House, which did not suit Kizzy's plans. 'Tell Admiral Twiss I will come if he wants me,' said Miss Brooke as she let Kizzy out.

Why should the Admiral want her? He, Peters, Nat, Kizzy did not want anybody on Saturdays and Sundays; and why did Miss Brooke look grave – and as if she were sorry? Why should she be sorry? For a moment a cold little puzzlement touched Kizzy, then she shook it off; if Miss Brooke were in trouble she was sorry but this was Saturday – and tomorrow . . . With the blanket on her shoulder, the carrier bag bumping against her legs, Kizzy set off for the stables, and stopped.

Usually she went straight to the stables and meadow. Later on she and Nat would go to the House and have cocoa in the kitchen with Peters. Usually Kizzy did not see the Admiral till lunchtime and not always then – often he stayed in his workshop – but this morning he was in the stable yard, waiting. Waiting for me . . . and Kizzy's heart seemed to skip a beat. He did not call out to her, but waited and, as she came up to him, she saw that the look on his face was the same as Miss Brooke's, grave and sorry – sorry to sadness.

Then Kizzy was frightened, more frightened than when Mr Blount had come and taken her to school, or when Peters fetched her and Gran was dead, when the wagon was burned and the Does talked about her and Joe, when she dared take Joe to the Admiral, or when she was sent to Miss Brooke and when the girls caught her on her way from school. As she looked up at the Admiral, her eyes were stretched wide with fear. 'Kiz,' said the Admiral. 'It's Joe.'

'Joe?' It came out as a gasp.

Admiral Twiss never dodged, but said things plainly. 'Joe died last night, Kiz. He is dead.'

Dead. The gravel seemed to tilt under Kizzy's feet, the stable cupola to run up into the sky. She dropped the blanket and bag. Admiral Twiss steadied her and brought her to the old mounting block.

'Nat went to give him his hay at seven o'clock and found Joe with his head hanging, dozing. Nat gave him a pat and held out some sugar, but Joe did not look at it, then he went down on his knees. Nat ran and got some beer.'

'Joe – liked – beer.' The words seemed to be torn from Kizzy.

'But, again, he wouldn't look. Then Nat said he rolled over on the grass and was dead.'

'Was – he – ill?'

'No,' said the Admiral, 'but he was old – and tired. Nat says his teeth were all worn down, which was why we couldn't fatten him, but Joe died in his own time, Kiz; not many horses do that, and in his meadow on his own grass where he had lived.'

'Show me him,' said Kizzy.

'Show a child a sight like *that*!' Mrs Cuthbert was

indignant when she heard. 'Trust a man to do such a thing.'

'You can trust the Admiral,' said Miss Brooke. 'He knows Kizzy wouldn't have believed him else.'

'But to let her see such a sight!'

Joe had not been a sight. When Admiral Twiss took Kizzy to him, he was lying peacefully in the grass. Kizzy held the Admiral's hand.

Nat came out, took Kizzy's other hand and together the three of them stood looking at the big still body, at Joe's head with the white blaze on his nose, his eyelashes – Nat had closed his eyes – his great legs and mighty hooves that were split and grey – it was a long while since he had worn shoes. His bay coat still shone, Nat had given it many a rubbing; Joe seemed as if he were asleep, but deep deep asleep.

Kizzy went nearer. 'Careful,' said Nat. 'He's getting stiff.'

'Will – will the knacker, the hounds, get him now?'

'They can't,' said Admiral Twiss.

'Can't?' Kizzy's head came up.

'Joe's safe,' said the Admiral, 'because this isn't Joe. He's not here.'

Kizzy broke from him and put her hand to Joe's nose, not touching him. 'He doesn't huff,' she said.

'Of course not. He isn't there.'

Kizzy looked at the Admiral as if weighing what he

105

said and put down her hand again to Joe. 'The warm is gone.'

'Yes.' Admiral Twiss came to her and gently touched Joe's body. 'This is just his old clothes, Kiz. He doesn't need them any more.'

'Where is he?'

Mrs Blount might have said, 'In the horses' heaven,' but Admiral Twiss was plainer. 'We don't know. Nobody knows, but I believe we shall find out.'

'When we're dead?'

'Perhaps. It seems to make sense, doesn't it?' said the Admiral. 'If Joe isn't here, he must be somewhere else. Come. We'll leave his body to Nat.'

'Shall I go to the House this morning?' Kizzy asked Miss Brooke on Sunday.

'Of course.'

For what, Kizzy could have asked, but, as if she had, 'Admiral Twiss and Peters are there,' said Miss Brooke, 'and Nat, and there are other horses.'

That was what Nat said. 'You have to swaller this.' Kizzy, almost automatically, had gone to him in the stables where he was hosing down Flavius, a colt who had a swollen leg. 'Swaller it down. Joe was a hoss and, like it or not, hosses won't last you all your life. They come and they go; dealin' with hosses you have to learn that. Near broke my heart, I did, when Royal went at Beechers.'

'Beechers?'

106

'The jump in the Grand National, stupid. What a jump! Feels as if you drop twenty feet. Must clear the water. He went in; had to pull him out with ropes but his neck was broke. Royal and Taggart – reared him by hand I did – and Bonbon; used to put her nose in my pocket for sugar, and did she nip if there wasn't any. Right spoiled she was; peppermint creams too, but blest me if she didn't get moon blindness; went blind bit by bit, so she had to be put down. You have to swaller it.'

Admiral Twiss said the same, 'I lost Rainbird,' and said it of his grandmother, Kezia. 'She had an Arab mare, a white one called Silver. Silver used to come up the front steps for sugar and followed her like a dog.'

'What happened to Silver?'

'Broke a leg out hunting.'

'What happened?'

'Had to be shot.' The Admiral said it abruptly as if he could not bear to think of it even now and Kizzy put her hands over her ears – she seemed to hear that shot – but, 'You have to swaller it,' said Nat and, 'Come along and give me a hand with Meadowsweet.'

He was pulling the filly's tail: 'Shaping it,' said Nat. The long hairs came out one by one in his nimble hands while Meadowsweet fidgeted, tossed her head, pretended to bite – and did nothing, even when Nat let Kizzy try. 'Doesn't hurt her, only tickles, if you take a firm hold and give a quick firm pull down.'

Afterwards he let Kizzy lead Meadowsweet back to the paddock. "'S the only thing to do. Go on to the next one.'

'Did Kezia – did your grandmother have another horse after Silver?' Kizzy asked the Admiral.

'Bless me, yes. Silver was one of a long long line of hunters,' and the Admiral said what Nat said, 'You have to go on to the next one.'

They all seemed to have forgotten that Kizzy had no next one.

'I think you will find they won't touch you again,' Miss Brooke said on Monday when she dropped Kizzy at school. 'In fact I'm sure of it,' and did not dream how right she was.

Everyone looked at the mark on Kizzy's forehead; the girls gave it surreptitious glances in the classroom; it was like a visible scolding, but no one spoke of it – and no one spoke to Kizzy, except Mrs Blount, and Mr Fraser in the playground at breaktime; he made a point of coming there and found Kizzy sitting by herself on the steps with a book. 'All right again, Kizzy?'

'Yes sir,' but it was not all right; there seemed to be a magic circle drawn round Kizzy, invisible, and no girl crossed it; when she came out to go home, two boys, Stephen and Tommy, smaller than Clem, who did not come out until half past three, were waiting at the gate; Stephen walked one side of her, Tommy on the other.

'You needn't,' said Kizzy.

'Clem said we was to,' and they plodded on. Next day it was Robert and George. The girls watched but none of them taunted or sang an insult out. 'Mr Fraser must have ordered the boys to do that,' they said among themselves; it made them feel more than ever under a cloud and they kept away from Kizzy as she kept away from them. At break and after-dinner-play, when the boys were in a separate playground, Kizzy sat on her step with the largest book she could find; she could almost read now – Miss Brooke helped her in the evenings – but everyone knew she certainly could not read the Encyclopaedia Britannica; she took a volume because they were the largest books in the classroom.

Once Mary Jo, playing hop-scotch, called 'Come and hop . . . Kizzy,' but Elizabeth Oliver whispered, 'Silly, she doesn't know how to play.' Kizzy put down her book, walked to the chalked-out space; she gave a withering look at Elizabeth, cast her pebble, hopped neatly and exactly from square to square, then 'home' without one fault; her legs were far stronger than theirs. Then she walked back to her place, sat down and buried herself in her book. Even at dinner there seemed to be a little iceberg of silence each side of her. It was not that she was ostracized now; it was simply uncomfortable to be near her. Somehow neither she, nor the other children could begin – except Clem. He often came at weekends to Amberhurst House – the Admiral liked him more and more – and sometimes in the week to tea at the cottage. 'You ought to ask Kizzy back,' said his mother.

'She wouldn't come.'

'Surely . . .', but, 'No, thank you,' said Kizzy steadily. Mrs Cuthbert too asked her to tea or to spend the day with Prue, but Kizzy went into such panic that Miss Brooke had to promise she need not go, 'Not ever, promise. Promise,' begged Kizzy. Yet she was feeling lonely. Funny; when she was in the orchard, solitary except for Gran, she had never felt alone; now, in the middle of girls and boys, she knew sharply what loneliness was. She walked to school by herself and soon by herself walked home – when Clem was sure she was safe from Prue's gang, he had released the boys.

It was not only school; in those warm summer days, May, June, July, Miss Brooke would find Kizzy standing at the open window, 'gazing,' she told the Admiral. Once she put her arm round Kizzy and said, 'I wish I could help you, Kiz.' Kizzy leant against her, rubbed her curls against Miss Brooke's shoulder – 'She would never have done that a few weeks ago,' – 'I wish I could help.'

'You do,' said Kizzy, but it was such a weary little voice that, 'I knew I didn't,' Miss Brooke told the

110

Admiral, and she said, 'Something must be done to heal this.'

'You wouldn't consider,' Miss Brooke asked Admiral Twiss, 'letting Kizzy, one Saturday, ask the girls in her class to tea at the House?'

'*Those* girls!' the Admiral recoiled.

'Those girls among them. I would willingly ask them to the cottage but it wouldn't be the same as coming to the House to see your models and the horses – it would give Kizzy an importance.'

'But ask girls, *those* girls, to Amberhurst.' The Admiral was stunned.

'It's a wonderful idea,' said Mr Fraser when he was consulted. 'Nothing could help Kizzy more.'

'If you really think so . . .' Admiral Twiss could be talked round, but not the gnomes, Peters and Nat. Not Kizzy.

'Put on a tea for those bullies. Not on your life,' said Peters.

'They're only little girls,' pleaded Miss Brooke.

'Little girls. Little monsters. Fourteen against one.'

'Let a pack of children near my youngsters. No, Admiral *Sir*,' said Nat while Kizzy, when the idea was broached, said, 'I might ask the boys.'

'But it's not the boys, it's the girls who need . . .' began Miss Brooke.

'I should have to ask Prue . . .' Kizzy breathed through her nostrils – like a little war horse or dragon, thought Miss Brooke. 'If Sir Admiral lets those girls come to the House,' said Kizzy, 'I'll never go there again.'

'Kizzy, don't you see, you have to make the first move because you were the one who was hurt?'

'I'll stay hurt,' said Kizzy.

Miss Brooke gave up the idea and the loneliness went on; it was like a hard shell round Kizzy that nobody could break.

The summer holidays came and, with them, brilliant weather. 'What are you and Kizzy going to do?' Mrs Cuthbert asked Miss Brooke.

'Oh, picnic and garden.'

'Here?'

'Where else?'

'You should get away.'

'I don't think Kizzy is quite ready for that.' Miss Brooke did not explain that she had spent so much money buying extra things for Kizzy she could not afford to go away.

'Look,' said Mrs Cuthbert. 'You go, Olivia, and we'll take Kizzy to the seaside with us.'

'It's very good of you, Edna . . .'

'She can sleep with Prue . . .'

Miss Brooke could almost hear Kizzy saying, 'I'll climb out of the window first.'

'It's good of you, Edna,' Miss Brooke repeated, 'but

112

it might spoil your holiday. Besides, I don't think Kizzy would go.'

'Heavens, you don't have to ask her.'

'I think I do. People should always be asked before being disposed of.'

'A child.'

'Children are people, Edna,' said Miss Brooke as she had said it to Mrs Blount.

'Well, please yourself,' said Mrs Cuthbert. 'But I tell you, Olivia, that child's too much on your mind.'

'Isn't that what she came for?'

'For what?'

'To be on my mind.'

'Peters,' said Admiral Twiss on a close hot morning in August. 'I was thinking. It must be stifling in that little thatched cottage of Miss Brooke's.'

'It must, sir.'

The spacious rooms of the House were cool; the lawns stretched invitingly to the park where the trees gave a deep shade. 'I was thinking if I asked Kizzy – and Miss Brooke to stay,' he said it with a rush – 'until this hot spell was over, what would you say?'

Peters said nothing but began to clear away.

'Would you . . . object?'

'It's not for me to object, sir,' said Peters, who had objected so often before.

'She could have the blue room.' The blue room had

been the Admiral's mother's and Kezia, his grand-mother's.

'So she could, sir.'

'Tell Nat,' said the Admiral and, putting on his panama, in his thin alpaca jacket and light trousers, he walked down the village to the cottage and, for the first time, saw Miss Brooke troubled.

'It would be lovely,' she had said when he asked her, 'but . . .'

'But what?'

'True, it is very hot here,' said Miss Brooke. 'I should be grateful if you would have Kizzy. She would love it but . . . I had better not.'

'I see,' said the Admiral slowly. 'It's Mrs Cuthbert.'

'All the Mrs Cuthberts,' said Miss Brooke.

'Tittle-tattle,' said Admiral Twiss crossly.

'You can't blame them,' said Miss Brooke.

'Kizzy can't come to tea with us,' Mrs Cuthbert had said – and Mary Jo's mother and Sally's and Elizabeth's. 'But I notice she can always go to the House.' 'It's the House, the House, the House,' they said.

Once Mrs Cuthbert had lost her temper. 'Olivia, I never knew you were a snob. Yes, it makes my blood boil,' said Mrs Cuthbert. 'My Prudence not good enough for a gypsy brat.'

'Don't be silly, Edna.' Miss Brooke was still calm. 'You know it isn't that and Kizzy's not a brat. She's shy of other children, that's all, and think, Edna – she

114

came to me from the House, where they were more than good to her. Naturally she loves them, especially Admiral Twiss.'

'Which is why he comes to visit her so often – at your cottage.'

'Gossiping about us, eh?' asked the Admiral now.

'Indeed yes.' Miss Brooke raised her candid hazel eyes. 'They think I'm in love with you – and you wouldn't like to encourage that, would you?' asked Miss Brooke.

School began again in September and again, every day, Kizzy stayed in her circle or private shell and no one broke in. Then one afternoon she came back to find Miss Brooke sweeping up leaves, fallen twigs and garden rubbish into a bonfire and, 'Couldn't we have tea out here, Olivia?' begged Kizzy.

'You let her call you Olivia,' Mrs Cuthbert had said.

'What else is she to call me? "Miss Brooke" seems so stiff.'

'Auntie Olivia.'

'I am not her aunt.'

'Couldn't we, Olivia? Have tea here?'

'In the vegetable patch?'

'The vegetables don't matter. It's the fire.'

The wind was chilly, the days were closing in and Miss Brooke hesitated. 'I'll show you how to keep warm.' Kizzy was excited. She brought a piece of

115

corrugated iron left over from the chicken house. 'We'll put it up here with some bricks to hold it.' More bricks, with the ironing board across them, made a bench. 'I used to have a box to sit on,' said Kizzy. 'If only we had Gran's kittle iron.'

'What's that?'

'You dig it into the ground to make it stand over the fire and hang the kettle on it. Prob'ly it's still in the orchard. Tomorrow I'll go and look.' For the moment they used Miss Brooke's picnic methylated stove for the kettle and fried bacon and sausages – rather burned bacon and sausages – over the fire in an old frying pan. Kizzy put apples on a stone and roasted them. 'Tastes good out of doors,' said Kizzy and Miss Brooke had to admit it. Chuff came out to bear them company and had his saucer of milk there. When it grew dark, Kizzy fetched two sacks, one for Miss Brooke, one for herself. 'We put 'em over our shoulders,' and they sat there in the garden, with the fire on their faces, the stars overhead.

Kizzy sang for Miss Brooke in a low crooning voice, unexpectedly sweet. Miss Brooke had never heard her sing, nor did she know the songs.

> 'Come along, my little gypsy girl,
> Come along with me, I pray.
> A-stealing horses we shall go
> Over the hill and far away.

Before your mother and your aunt
I'll down upon my knee,
And beg they'll give me their little girl
To be my Romady.'

'Better you should a-tinkering go
And I should fortunes tell.
For then safe in our little tent
Contented we might dwell.'

'Well said, my little gypsy girl,
I like well what you say.
We'll tinker and we'll fortune tell
Over the hills and far away.'

'Who taught you that?'
'My Gran,' and Kizzy sang again.

Oh! the eggs and bacon;
And oh! the eggs and bacon;
And the gentleman and lady
   A walking up the way!
And if you will be my sweetheart,
And if you will be my sweetheart,
And if you will be my darling,
   I will be your own, today.

Oh! I found a jolly hedgehog;
Oh! I found a good fat hedgehog;

Oh! I found a good big hedgehog,
  In the wood beyond the town:
And there came the lord and lady,
The handsome lord and lady,
And underneath the branches
  I saw the two sit down.

They didn't know the Gypsy,
They didn't think the Gypsy,
They didn't hear the Gypsy
  Was looking — or could hide.
If they knew I saw the kisses,
The pretty little kisses,
If they knew I heard the kisses,
  Oh, the lady would ha' died! . . .

'Can I have my tea here every day?' asked Kizzy.

'And she was happy,' Miss Brooke told Admiral Twiss.

'Ah!' said the Admiral.

'But you *said* . . .' Kizzy stopped in the cottage doorway, flushed with running and disappointment. 'You said we should have tea by the bonfire,' yet there was Miss Brooke with the tea table drawn up to the sitting-room fire.

It was a month later. Through the end of September, and first weeks of October, they had had tea in the garden, 'when it wasn't absolutely deluging,' said

Miss Brooke. Kizzy had found the kittle iron, though it was heavy to lug from the orchard, and Miss Brooke set it up; the Does had taken the kettle but Miss Brooke found an old one. The sheltering sheet of iron had been made steady and a plank found for a bench instead of the ironing board; Miss Brooke had found a wooden box and it, too, had lettering on it: *McGregor Dundee*. Kizzy came home every day to see smoke going up, the kettle on the boil. 'I think tea does taste better in the open air,' said Miss Brooke.

'Olivia,' said Kizzy solemnly. 'I think I love you.'

Once Mrs Cuthbert almost caught them. They heard her knock, but Miss Brooke had locked the front door so that Mrs Cuthbert could not come in with her usual bounce; the only way into the garden was through the house or the garage – that was locked too – 'and the hedges pen us in,' Miss Brooke said. She went to open the door for Mrs Cuthbert. 'Why, Olivia, your hair's all ends. You look thoroughly windblown. What *have* you been doing?'

'Having tea in the garden.'

'Tea in the garden! In this gale and cold!'

'We were not cold.'

'I do love you,' Kizzy had said when Miss Brooke came back, but now . . . 'You *said* I should have tea in the garden,' she accused.

'You are having tea in the garden.'

'But you . . .'

'You won't need me,' said Miss Brooke. 'Go out and look.'

Kizzy went into the garden – but it was not the garden she had left that morning with its narrow flagged terrace edged with lavender, its square of grass – 'my pocket handkerchief lawn,' Miss Brooke called it – that sloped down to the vegetable patch which was bounded by a high hedge overgrown with honeysuckle; the chicken house was in the corner opposite the built-out L of Miss Brooke's bedroom where the thatch came past her dormer window low to the ground. The terrace, the lavender and the hedge were still there, but the chicken house and vegetables were gone, 'spirited away' Kizzy could have said had she known those words. Indeed, it seemed as if elf hands had been at work. 'Funny sort of elves,' Nat would have chuckled. 'Me and old Peters and the Admiral – worked like slaves we did. Everything brought at dead of night in the horsebox lorry and hidden in the garage so the Paul Prys wouldn't see. Anyway, those who were awake were glued to the telly,' but it was magic to Kizzy.

Below the small lawn, what had been the vegetable patch was turfed now, and planted with trees that made a screen from the house, little bush apple trees, not much higher than Kizzy's head, but there were apples on them, rosy ones; she put out a finger and touched one. It was real, with a real smell. Apple trees cannot be planted when they are in fruit, but Miss

Brooke had skilfully threaded small red apples with fine string and tied them to the trees, so that they looked as if they were growing on them. Through the trees Kizzy could see firelight – 'and somethin' else,' whispered Kizzy. On tiptoe with wonder she stepped between the apple trees that, she saw now, made a little orchard round a clearing where a fire had been built, not a heaped bonfire like Miss Brooke's, but a proper cooking fire built in a hollow. Over the fire was a kittle iron, not big and heavy like Gran's, but 'small enough for me,' and from it hung a stout doll-size kettle from which a plume of steam was coming out; when she saw the steam Kizzy's knees went weak with wonder. The shelter had become half-size, with a half-size bench, a smaller box, and, drawn up to the fire, was a wagon, a true real wagon, exactly like Gran's, 'only hers was so shabby.' This was new and painted blue and green with a carved and gilded front, its wheels hooped with iron; its bottom half-door was shut, the top half open, a flight of steps led up to it, all the right size for Kizzy, a child's wagon; no grown-up could come into it. Even Miss Brooke, small as she was, could only have put her head in or else bent double.

There were crisp muslin curtains at the windows and window boxes with earth in them. 'They are planted with bulbs – miniature bulbs,' said Miss Brooke, who had followed Kizzy out. 'Tiny daffodils and tulips. In spring they will come out.' A line of washing was stretched between two apple trees, 'like ours used to do,' hung with Kizzy's jeans and socks and a small apron held by doll clothes pegs. The shafts were lowered into the grass; the only thing missing was the net of hay for Joe that Gran had kept slung under the wagon.

Inside the wagon a light was burning and, going up the steps, Kizzy could see a lamp with a pink shade just like Gran's, only the lamp was six inches high. There were two bunks — 'as there were for Gran and me,' — with pillows and blankets and patchwork quilts. 'Can — can I sleep here?' 'When it's warmer,' said Miss Brooke. There was a child-size table and chair — Gran had had a chair — a strip of carpet, a postcard-size mirror and, on a shelf, a set of china, white with pink roses, doll-size. 'They belonged to the Admiral's grandmother,' said Miss Brooke. 'Kezia!' whispered Kizzy.

A small saucepan and frying pan hung side by side: 'I can make a pan fried cake.' There were china ornaments and a doll vase of the plastic flowers Kizzy thought so beautiful. A twig broom stood in the corner. 'We didn't need a dustpan. We just swept dust outside, but we did need a bucket.' There was a small bucket, 'There's . . . everything,' whispered Kizzy.

The wagon in the firelight threw its shadow on the grass — a child-size shadow; the lamplight shone through the windows in the dusk. Kizzy gave a long sigh, a sigh of happiness. 'It's mine.'

Chapter Six

The Court had been hearing a case of damage at the village school by 'two young hooligans', said Mr Blount and, 'As we are all here again,' said the Chairman, 'tell us – the traveller child, Kizzy Lovell, is she happy and well?' and he asked, 'Miss Brooke? Mr Blount?'

'Would you like me to leave while you discuss her?' asked Miss Brooke.

'There isn't anything to discuss,' said Mr Blount. 'Kizzy is well and putting on weight. She seems to conform now without any difficulty, though she keeps to herself – that's perhaps because of an unfortunate episode after school . . .'

'What episode?' Mrs Cuthbert, who was there representing the School Board, was instantly alert.

'It seems some of the children set on her, the girls . . .'

'Well, it certainly wasn't my Prudence . . . and, may I ask, why were we not told?'

'Mr Fraser thought it better to let the children settle it themselves – which they have done,' and

123

before Mrs Cuthbert could speak again Mr Blount went hurriedly on. 'Kizzy can read now. Miss Brooke has been coaching her in the holidays and evenings. She is beautifully kept. I feel, sir,' he said to the Chairman, 'Miss Brooke should be congratulated; it might all have been most difficult.'

'It isn't finished yet,' said Miss Brooke. Indeed, Mrs Cuthbert spoke to her afterwards.

'I didn't say this in the courtroom because I didn't want to shame you, Olivia, but I don't believe you are making such a success of that child. If there's another opportunity, I shall feel bound to speak.'

'Is that a threat?' asked Miss Brooke, smiling.

'Olivia Brooke! As if I would threaten, but that little girl is too solitary.'

'I quite agree.'

'Then why do you let her be? The fact is, Olivia, you have become possessive. That's what I meant when I said a single woman shouldn't take a child. Possessive.'

'What do I do?' asked Miss Brooke.

'Keep her away from everybody – except the House, of course. If any of *us* ask her out you won't let her come, never let her ask any child near.'

Miss Brooke's lips twitched. 'Wouldn't it be nice, Kizzy,' she had said some days ago, 'if you invited some of the girls to see your orchard and wagon?'

'It would be horrid.'

'Just one or two,' coaxed Miss Brooke.

'No.'

'They would be fascinated.'

'No.'

'Think of showing them the Kezia china.'

'*No!*' – 'And Kizzy got into a state worse than when I suggested asking them to the House,' Miss Brooke told the Admiral. 'Yet I feel I must try.'

'Don't,' said Admiral Twiss. 'Let her be.'

Clem had been allowed to see – 'If you won't tell,' said Kizzy. 'Promise not to tell, not even Elizabeth. Particularly not Elizabeth.'

'I promise,' said Clem.

'Say "May I die if I lie".' Kizzy was fierce.

'May I die if I lie,' said Clem meekly.

'But mean it. Mean it. Mean it,' stormed Kizzy.

No one, absolutely no one was to know. 'But there are some queer goings-on,' said Mrs Cuthbert.

As soon as Kizzy came back from school, she and Miss Brooke would light her fire and boil the kettle. She taught Miss Brooke some of the gypsy ways with fires: 'Set them going,' said Kizzy, 'with bits of torn paper, or twigs, dried leaves; put a match to them – Gran used her flint – then build a sort of little chimney with twigs, thin, thin twigs. That pulls the fire up and then you put on branches; apple and willow burns quick; Gran said oak is good and slow, but we never had any oak; chestnut is bad, it snaps. Sir Admiral sometimes gave Gran elm logs. Elm is best.' Sometimes Kizzy fried her own bacon and sausages, roasted potatoes and apples but, even if Miss Brooke cooked it, always had her tea out there. Afterwards she would sit on her box or, if it rained, go into the wagon and light the little lamp. Miss Brooke would hear her singing and crooning to herself as she fed the fire or just sat dreaming, Chuff beside her. Chuff too had adopted the fire. Sometimes Kizzy brushed him, sometimes read the big print of her reading books; often she strung beads.

She had all the travellers' love of ornaments and colours. Miss Brooke had given her a box of old beads and Kizzy spent hours stringing them into necklaces and bracelets. 'She would go to school wearing six necklaces if I would let her,' said Miss Brooke. Kizzy longed to have a ring – like the Admiral's signet ring or, better, like one that Miss Brooke sometimes wore, with a moonstone and rubies.

'O bring me back my gold,'

Kizzy would sing,

> *'No gold ever ties me.*
> *Bring me back my gold*
> *'n the little diamint ring.'*

From the upstairs windows Miss Brooke watched and listened.

As the weather grew colder, 'Kizzy, it's time to

come in,' she would call from the window or garden door.

'Just a little longer. The stars are coming out. There's one enormous star; prob'ly it's Gran,' – Kizzy had a fixed idea that people turned into stars when they died – 'Might be Joe,' said Kizzy. It comforted her to think the star was Joe. 'I do need a pony,' she told his star. 'You would be too big for the wagon but you could come along.'

Sometimes Miss Brooke found her asleep on the box or in the wagon's bunk. Though Miss Brooke was slight, she was strong; she gathered Kizzy up, carried her indoors and upstairs and put her straight under the blankets into bed. Mrs Cuthbert caught her once. 'Olivia! You're too small to carry that great child up to bed.'

'She's not very heavy,' and, 'Don't wake her,' said Miss Brooke.

'But bed without washing!'

'She can have a bath in the morning.'

'Bed in her clothes!'

'She'll have clean ones tomorrow.'

The clothes smelled of wood smoke but that was Kizzy's familiar smell. 'What *has* she been doing?'

'Amusing herself.'

'At this hour! And you let her.'

'Yes,' said Miss Brooke.

'As I said before, you have queer ways of bringing up a child.'

'*Is* it too queer?' Miss Brooke asked Admiral Twiss. 'We are encouraging her in make-believe.'

'Yes,' said Admiral Twiss, 'but make-believe is a good splint for a break, and a good many things have been broken for Kizzy.'

It was bonfire night. A huge bonfire had been built on the common. "S'almost as tall as a house,' said Clem. For weeks the older boys and girls had been trundling their guys in old perambulators and wooden handcarts round the village and even into Rye, wheedling money for fireworks. 'Penny for the guy. Two pennies. Five pence,' and now all the children were seething with excitement, except Kizzy.

'You're coming, Kiz?' said Clem.

'No.'

'There'll be fireworks,' said Clem. 'Not just our own but big fireworks: rockets and Catherine wheels – they go round and round with flashes – and golden rain – you put bombs on the ground and they make fountains. There'll be crackers – back-a-rappers we call them. They chase you – and I got a whole packet of sparklers specially for you; you hold one in your hand and they go fizz in sparks. They don't hurt you. And there'll be stalls for hot dogs and toffee apples and candyfloss and we roast potatoes.'

'No.'

'Why, Kiz?'

'They burn the guy. I don't like that.'

128

'Don't be silly. He's not real. It's only fun.'

'Fun! All of you against one.' Kizzy said it bitterly.

'Aw! Come *on*!' said Clem. 'Besides, it's tit for tat. Guy Fawkes, he tried to blow up the Houses of Parliament.'

'Tit for tat.' Kizzy liked the sound of that. 'One day I'll blow up the whole school.'

'Then you'll be a skunk,' said Clem. 'Lots of them have been kind to you, the boys, Mr Fraser, especially Mrs Blount – hasn't she?'

Kizzy would not answer and, for the first time, Clem lost patience. He seized her by the arm and gave her a barley sugar twist, and not a gentle one. 'Hasn't she?'

'Y-es,' it was wrung from Kizzy.

'Hasn't Mr Fraser?'

'Y-es.'

'Haven't I, and the boys?'

'Y-es.'

'Well then. Why?'

'Them,' said Kizzy briefly.

'Look, Kiz,' said Clem. 'You have to make it up.'

'No.'

'You can't go on and on.'

'I can.'

'You can't,' said Clem. 'You'll see.'

Miss Brooke had meant to cajole Kizzy into coming to the bonfire with her, but when Kizzy came home it was to find her sick and giving involuntary little moans; the skin round her eyes was discoloured, 'and you're all yellow,' said Kizzy, alarmed.

'It's just one of my bad sick headaches,' Miss Brooke managed to say. 'It will be better if I lie down.'

Kizzy helped her upstairs to her quiet bedroom over the L, pulled back the counterpane and covered her with blankets. She made a cup of tea and carried it carefully up and brought Miss Brooke the pills she ought to have taken before. 'Only I wanted you to see the bonfire.'

'I like my own bonfire,' said Kizzy and pulled the curtains. 'Go to sleep.'

'Your tea . . .'

'I'll get my own tea – and feed Chuff.'

'You ought to see the fireworks . . .'

'Never mind them – unless they hurt your poor head. They're only bangs,' said Kizzy and soon Miss Brooke, who had been awake and sick most of the night, was in a deep sleep.

'Only bangs,' but, sitting on her box, Kizzy felt strangely forlorn and lonely; perhaps it was because Miss Brooke was not there, perhaps because of the excited voices coming from the common on the other side of the cottage, laughter and shouting and the sound of running footsteps. 'Sparklers, crackers, back-a-rappers, golden rain,' she whispered the magic-sounding words to Chuff and thought she caught a tang of gunpowder mingled with the smell of hot dogs on the air. She had half a mind to go to the front gate and watch.

When it was beginning to be dark a rocket whizzed into the sky and fell in a shower of stars that shone red as Miss Brooke's rubies in the dusk; they were more beautiful than anything Kizzy had ever seen – the orchard had been too far away from the village for her to have watched fireworks. Another rocket went up, blue and green: 'Sapphires 'n' emeralls,' whispered Kizzy to Chuff but Chuff, who disliked firework bangs, had run into the cottage. Kizzy went through the sitting room and out to the front gate.

'Lizbeth,' Clem coaxed his sister. 'Go to Miss Brooke's cottage and make Kizzy come and join us.'

'You go.'

'She won't come for me – because of you girls.'

'She won't come for us.'

'I believe she would if you asked her. Anyway, try. Go on, Lizbeth. You and Mary Jo.'

Elizabeth considered. 'It would have to be Prudence.'

'Prue's the one she hates.'

'That's why,' said Elizabeth, but was still doubtful.

'Tell you what,' said Clem. 'If you make them go and Kizzy comes, I'll give you my new pencil box . . . 'sides, you want to make it up. You know you do,' and that was how three little girls met Kizzy at the garden gate.

Kizzy held the gate tight shut. 'We haven't come to fight,' said Elizabeth.

'Why have you then?' Kizzy was breathing through her nose, again like a little dragon.

'Fains, Kizzy.' Prudence offered the truce and, 'We came to ask you along to the bonfire with us,' said Mary Jo, and, 'Please come,' Elizabeth pleaded.

For a moment Kizzy's heart leapt, then the shell came down. 'I got a bonfire of my own,' she said loftily.

'You couldn't have, not like ours.'

'Better than yours.'

'Show.'

'Private,' said Kizzy.

'Then we don't believe you,' said Prue.

Kizzy looked at them; her eyes flashed – 'Black,' Elizabeth told Clem afterwards – and she threw open the garden gate. 'Come . . .'

'Oh!' 'O-oh!' 'O-ooh!' Elizabeth, Mary Jo and Prudence stood in the little orchard gazing at the apple trees with their rosy apples, the fire where the kettle was steaming, the lit wagon showing a glimpse of windows and curtains and china. 'O-ooo-ooooh!'

'It's a wendy-house caravan,' said Elizabeth.

'Never seen anythin' like it.'

'And it's yours?'

132

Kizzy nodded. She was swelling with pride. 'You can go into the wagon if you like.'

Reverently they went up the steps and the bonfire on the common was forgotten.

'Look at the little pillows!'

'Real patchwork quilts.'

'Why two bunks?'

'So's I can ask a friend to spend the night.'

'Do you sleep here then?'

'Sometimes,' said Kizzy.

'She lets you?'

'When I like.'

'Wish I could,' said Elizabeth.

'Maybe one day I'll ask you.'

'China's right pretty,' said Mary Jo.

'It's a hundred years old,' said Kizzy. 'Belonged to Kezia Cunningham at the House,' and she boasted, 'I'm called after her.'

'Then Admiral Twiss made this for you?'

'Yes, he's a friend of mine.' Kizzy felt she was getting bigger and bigger.

'But you need a pony,' said Prue.

'The pony hasn't come yet.'

'You're going to have a *pony*!'

'Make you some tea if you like.' Kizzy thought they had better stop talking about the pony. 'Kettle's boiling,' which drew their attention to the fire and, for the first time, Prudence criticized. ''S a very little fire.'

'Has to be,' said Elizabeth, 'to match.'

'She said it was big.'

'It can be,' said Kizzy. 'I can make it as big as I like.' Something inside her knew she was boasting even more, yet she went on, moving the kittle-iron and the kettle and throwing on armful after armful of wood.

'Now you have put it out,' said Prue.

'Haven't,' and Kizzy went to the garage and brought out Miss Brooke's spare tin of petrol.

'Kizzy, you can't put that on it. Petrol's dangerous.'

'Stand back,' was all Kizzy said.

She meant to sprinkle a few drops but the tin was heavy. Petrol gushed out and, 'Kizzy!' screamed Mary Jo as there was a bang and a flash of flame. Kizzy dropped the tin and jumped back as a sheet of fire came up. 'How it didn't catch her face I don't know,' said Elizabeth afterwards. In a moment there was what seemed a wall of fire with tongues reaching out towards the cottage; the thatch on the low eaves of the L caught at once, while the wind swept the fire upwards. Flames ran along the thatch and in a minute smoke began to come out of the upstairs windows. Chuff tore out of the house, his fur on end, and leaped, clawing, up the hedge.

The heat scorched the girls' faces and, 'The wagon! The little wagon,' screamed Elizabeth over the noise of the flames but, 'Never mind the wagon,' Kizzy shouted back. 'Olivia . . . Miss Brooke, she's asleep in there.' Before they could catch her, Kizzy had dodged

134

round the flames and dived into the smoking cottage. Elizabeth screamed; Mary Jo began to sob, but Prudence was not Mrs Cuthbert's daughter for nothing. 'Run, Beth,' she ordered. 'Run. Get Clem. Get men.'

'Better . . . ring . . . fire brigade,' choked Elizabeth.

'They would never believe children on bonfire night.' Prue was cool, decisive. 'Run!' and Elizabeth ran, dodging through the sitting room, which was not yet alight, but leaving the door open, which fanned the flames; the sitting room began to fill with smoke but Prudence was still cool. 'Mary Jo, come with me.'

'In *there*?'

'We got to. Got to get 'em out. *Come on*. Don't chicken.'

As they came into the cottage, they heard faint cries. 'We're coming,' shouted Prue but she did not, like Kizzy, dash straight up the stairs. She ran into the kitchen, found two glass cloths and held them under the tap. 'Tie this over your mouth and nose,' she commanded, giving one to Mary Jo. 'Tie it tight. Now come.'

'Up there?' Mary Jo quailed. ''S – moke.'

''Course. Come on.'

The stairs were a steep single cottage flight with a small landing at the top; smoke was billowing down them now, filling the sitting room. 'Crawl,' said Prue over her shoulder. They could hear Kizzy coughing and spluttering above them, then saw her frantically trying to pull Miss Brooke's body through an open door. Smoke belched out from behind her and as Prue, on her hands and knees, got to them, Kizzy choked, doubled up and fell. In one swift movement, Prue grabbed her curls; Kizzy was light, easy to pull clear and Prue passed her to Mary Jo. 'Throw her down the stairs.'

'*Throw?*' Their voices were muffled by the cloths.

'Yes. Quick.' Beyond Miss Brooke, Prue saw lumps of burning thatch fall through the ceiling, fire run along the ancient beams. '*Throw* her. Hurry!'

'She'll be hurt.'

'Never mind. Quick. Come *on. Come on!*'

Mary Jo's hurl sent limp light Kizzy head over heels down the stairs but Miss Brooke was another matter; though a slight woman, unconscious she was heavy for two small girls. 'Pull,' gasped Prue.

'Can't.' Mary Jo was coughing; both their eyes were red, streaming and smarting, half blinded; heat scorched their cheeks. 'Can't.'

'Must.' Prue set her teeth and, with all the strength of their short arms, they pulled and tugged Miss Brooke to the landing. 'Take – legs,' spluttered Prue and together they dragged her feet round. 'Go – down,' Mary Jo retreated down three steps. 'Pull – legs – pull,' gasped Prue.

The bedroom was ablaze now but Prue knelt at the head of the stairs and got Miss Brooke's head and shoulders up, heaving her own body beneath them. '*Pull.*' It was torn out of Prue, whose wet cloth had slipped. She took in a mouthful of smoke and choked. 'Pull.' Mary Jo caught the legs and Miss Brooke began to slither downwards.

Prue felt her own hair frizzle, a searing pain on her neck and saw her dress was alight; she gave a final frantic heave and Miss Brooke cascaded down, taking Mary Jo with her as running steps burst into the cottage; a man caught up Kizzy, a second Mary Jo as Prudence herself keeled over and tumbled down the flight right over Miss Brooke into a third man's arms; he seized the hearthrug and rolled Prue in it, smothering the flames on her dress. Two more men swung up Miss Brooke.

''Struth,' they said afterwards. 'We got them out just in time.'

'*We* got them out. It was young Prudence Cuthbert.'

'Where is she?'

The Admiral's old Rolls had come tearing into the village and he, Peters and Nat were out of it in a moment when it drew up with a shrieking of tyres outside the cottage. Two fire engines were there, firemen trampling over the garden, their hoses still jetting out water that sent a mushroom of smoke spreading over the sky with a terrible smell of charring. Some of the downstairs furniture had been carried out and stood higgledy-piggledy in the garden, soaked with dirty water and grimed with smoke. The excitement of the cottage on fire had dimmed the excitement of the bonfire and at least half the village was gathered there. Admiral Twiss went through them like a reap-hook through corn.

'How did he get here so soon?'

'Doctor was playing chess with him,' Nat explained. 'Hospital telephoned.'

'Where is she?' Looking at the Admiral's blanched face, a murmur went round. 'Lord, how he do love that child.'

'Is she alive? Hurt? Where is she?'

'Little girl's all right, sir.' The Chief Fireman came up. 'All the little girls. Overcome by smoke, of course. The ambulance has taken them to hospital. One has some burns but not severe.'

The Admiral still seemed dazed and a dozen voices reassured him. 'Kizzy's safe. She's all right. Kizzy is all right, sir.'

'No. No, not Kizzy,' said the Admiral. 'At least – Kizzy yes, but not Kizzy . . .' and in front of them all he cried, 'Where is *she*? Is *she* hurt? Olivia? Miss Brooke?'

'I told you she was setting her cap at him,' said Mrs Cuthbert. The village seldom remembered a more exciting time. Mary Jo and Kizzy were discharged from hospital next day and Kizzy went to stay with the Olivers, 'With Clem and Elizabeth,' said Kizzy. Prudence came out next; with her bandaged neck and hands she was the heroine of the village. 'Wouldn't be surprised if she got a medal,' and even Peters had to say, 'Got a head on her shoulders, that one.'

The cottage was a blackened half-ruin, sheeted with tarpaulins, the furniture stacked up. 'You can't live there now,' Admiral Twiss told Miss Brooke – he had gone straight to the hospital and was there every day. 'You and Kiz will have to come to Amberhurst.'

'But . . .'

'Talk. Yes, there will be talk.' The Admiral said it irritably, but his eyebrows did not bristle. 'But there's one way to stop it – if you will say "Yes", Olivia.'

'For Kizzy's sake . . .'

'Not Kizzy's – yours and mine. Kizzy too, of course, but when I thought you were burnt . . .' The Admiral's eyebrows and moustache worked so violently he had to go to the hospital window. 'It's no good. You will have to say "Yes", Olivia.'

'Yes,' said Miss Brooke. It was a little while later that she asked – and her eyes were laughing, 'How will you tell Nat and Peters?'

Chapter Seven

'My wagon was burned, just like Gran's. Then am I dead?' Kizzy had said when she came round in the hospital which was not at all like her idea of heaven. 'I must be dead.' But, though she was not to be a star just yet, in a way the old Kizzy was dead. 'I wouldn't go to the bonfire,' she confessed to the Admiral, 'and I was showing off.' She could hear herself boasting, see herself with the petrol can. 'I nearly killed Olivia.' She caught her breath. 'If Mary Jo and Prue . . .' He had told her what they had done. 'Brave little girls,' said Admiral Twiss, 'particularly Prudence.'

Particularly Prue. 'I'll ask her to sit next me,' said Kizzy with a gulp. 'If . . . if Clem will sit on my other side.'

Peters was icing a birthday cake in the big House kitchen, a white cake, three-tiered, that would presently be decorated with silver balls and red cherries. It was to have eight red candles and he had promised to write in chocolate icing: *Kezia Happy Birthday*.

'But I thought you said you wouldn't have anything to do with it,' said Kizzy.

'It's your birthday cake, ain't it?' asked Peters. 'You ain't ever had a cake before. Who else do you think I'd let make it? Come to that, you ain't ever had a birthday, let alone a party.'

'Then you don't mind about the party?'

'Mind or not mind, makes no difference.' Peters skilfully turned the cake. 'Let one woman in, you may as well let fifty.'

Lady Cunningham Twiss. Mrs Cuthbert could not make her tongue say it, could not 'swaller it', as Nat would have said. 'I think it's wonderful,' said Mrs Blount. 'To think it was Kizzy, that little traveller girl, who brought them together. They are adopting her. She will be Kezia Cunningham Twiss.'

Mrs Cuthbert could not swallow that either. 'And to think she came to my back door selling flowers! In a way I started it,' which was bitter.

'I suppose you have seen Olivia?' Mildred Blount went on.

'Indeed no. You'll find she'll have no use for us now. Lady Cunningham Twiss!'

The telephone rang. 'Edna?'

'It's Olivia!' Mrs Cuthbert whispered and said into the telephone, 'Yes, Olivia?' Her voice was guarded.

'We are giving a party,' said the voice on the

telephone, 'to say "thank you" to the village, especially to Prue, and also for Kizzy's birthday.'

'I didn't know you knew it.'

'We have given her another Kezia's – that's her name now. We're hoping all the children will come and perhaps, Edna, you and Mildred would come and help me.'

'At the *House*?' Mrs Cuthbert could not believe it. 'The House?'

'Yes.'

'Well, I never!' said Mrs Cuthbert when she put the telephone down. 'I wonder how she will square *that* with Mr Peters.'

Kizzy was worried. 'Olivia, what happens on a birthday? I know there'll be a wreath . . . I . . . don't want to wear a wreath with everybody watching.'

'Well, this time of the year there isn't much to make a wreath of.'

'Prob'ly be holly – it pricks,' said Kizzy in gloom. Almost the old closed look was back. 'And they will bump me and pull my hair. Wish I was four, not eight.'

'Well, they won't bump you or pull your hair nor make a wreath because the 9th is a Saturday, so there won't be any school.'

'Nor there will.' Kizzy was relieved yet still knitted her brows. 'But what happens?'

Olivia drew Kizzy to her. 'For birthdays you

usually wait and see, but first, as soon as you wake, you look under your pillow.'

Before it was light that Saturday, Kizzy looked, and there, mysteriously under her pillow, lay a small riding whip with a silver top and a scarlet tassel. 'What a funny thing to give me,' thought Kizzy, but she liked to hold it in her hand; she could pretend she was Kezia Cunningham – 'And that was only the beginning,' marvelled Kizzy.

She had breakfast with Olivia and the Admiral, and all round her place were parcels – again of 'funny things': a yellow jersey from Olivia: a pair of little string gloves from Peters and a small-size horse brush and curry-comb from Nat. 'So as I can help with the horses.' There was nothing from the Admiral but there were many many cards. 'The whole village must have sent them,' said Olivia. She and Kizzy spent half an hour setting them up on the hall chimney-shelf and in Kizzy's bedroom. Then came 'the solemn moment,' said Kizzy.

Admiral Twiss took her into the library and opened the big Bible. 'This is your birthday now and I shall write in your name.' Kizzy watched, scarcely breathing, while in his fine pointed writing he wrote 'Kezia Lovell Cunningham Twiss, December 9th, eight years old.'

'Lovell?' asked Kizzy.

'You are what you are,' said the Admiral.

'That's what Gran said.'

'She was right – and never stoop to pretend to be anything else. You should be proud to be a Lovell, and proud of your Gran.'

'I will be,' said Kizzy, her head up. 'I am.'

Nat's whistle was heard on the drive and, 'I believe Nat wants you,' said the Admiral. He took Kizzy's hand and opened the front door.

It was a cold clear morning and sunlight streamed in through the door – it seemed to Kizzy, from that moment, that the sun streamed in for ever. There was frost in the air – what Nat called 'finger-cold weather' – and on it Kizzy caught a whiff of something loved, familiar, the scent of horse and leather; for there, on the drive, Nat, trying to keep his smile in, was holding the prettiest pony Kizzy had ever seen, seen or imagined – a small bay pony, 'Twelve hands,' said the Admiral, 'or, rather, twelve two.' The pony's ears were cocked as he looked towards them, his dark mane and flowing tail well brushed out; his coat shone as did his new saddle and bridle, his silver bit, and he fidgeted his small hooves on the gravel. 'Now then. Now then,' said Nat.

'But . . . whose is he?' Kizzy was dazed.

'Well, he isn't mine,' said Nat. 'Nor the Admiral's, nor her ladyship's. I don't think Peters would ride him. I believe he is meant for you.'

Kizzy had her first ride that morning, in the railed school where Nat lunged the young horses; she walked the pony round as Admiral Twiss told her, trying to hold the reins properly, use her legs, do the exercises he taught her while Nat watched critically. 'Half an hour is enough,' said Admiral Twiss, 'but you must learn to put your pony away. Take off his saddle and bridle, then put on his halter. Give him some water and put him in his stall to cool off while you clean your tack.'

Kizzy had one moment of doubt – and did not voice it to the Admiral. 'Nat,' she said as she polished and polished the small saddle. 'Do you . . . do you think Joe would mind?'

'Mind what?'

'My having another?'

''Course not,' said Nat. 'He would like to think he had made you love all horses; besides, this ain't another Joe. He's Joey.'

'Joey.'

'And old Joe knows he's too big for your wagon. This pony fits.'

But, 'I haven't got a wagon now,' said Kizzy.

It was almost three o'clock, time for the party.

The party had brought another worry, a crease in Kizzy's happiness, but she kept it to herself until Olivia had said, 'What is the matter, Kizzy?'

'Nothing.'

'Something – tell me.'

'Olivia,' said Kizzy, 'when . . . when the girls at

145

school go to parties, they all wear dresses. I have lovely jerseys and skirts but – I haven't a dress.'

'Haven't you?'

'Of course, they're quite clean . . .'

'Haven't you?' Olivia said it again. Then, 'I should go upstairs and look.'

On the new white bed a dress was spread. The last dress Kizzy had owned had been the draggled strawberry pink cotton; this was of soft maroon cloth, its sleeves puffed white muslin with a white ruffle at the neck. The bodice was laced with blue and round the skirt ran a band of blue velvet. 'It's – it's – Kezia's dress!' breathed Kizzy.

'This Kezia's,' said Olivia.

The great drawing room had been opened for the grown-up guests; the children's tea was set in the dining room on the Admiral's long table, with another equally long beside it. Peters' cake was on a separate table with a wreath of holly round it. 'You see, you don't have to wear the wreath because it's round the cake,' said Olivia. There were sprays of holly down the tables and red crackers. After tea there would be games and a conjuror; then the Admiral was to set his tug, the *Elsie May*, going on the lake with its port and starboard lights shining, 'and its searchlight lit,' said Clem, who was to help. It would come to shore – 'I hope,' said the Admiral – with a cargo of sweets, a bag for every child.

'There's never been a party like this in the village,' said Clem.

'Nor at the House.' Peters had to admit it.

'At least not for a hundred years,' said Admiral Twiss.

Yet it made Kizzy uneasy, more and more uneasy. This was the sort of party given for Kezia Cunningham Twiss. Kizzy Lovell might have asked a few boys – and girls, thought Kizzy grudgingly – to come to her fire in the orchard – if she had had a fire and an orchard. In the old days when other travellers had drawn off the road to see Gran and camp in the orchard for the night, food had been shared round, mugs of tea made; then Gran had lit her pipe with the men and someone brought out a mouth organ or an old violin, or just tambourines, thought Kizzy, and everyone would sing. Often they danced against the darkness of trees and sky, with the fire stirred up as if the sparks were music. That was the kind of party she understood and, in the beauty of her new dress, she went and looked out of the window, away to where the Admiral's orchard lay over the line of trees. Wish I had my little orchard and my wagon, thought Kizzy. She was Kezia with a pony and a gracious spacious home, 'More like a little princess than the saucepot that you are,' as Peters said – yet the old gypsy yearning was there.

She turned back to the dining room, where Olivia, with Mrs Cuthbert, Mrs Blount and Mrs

Oliver, was putting food on the tables – sandwiches, crisps, jellies, meringues – and folding little red napkins at the long line of places for the children. 'Wish they wasn't coming,' muttered Kizzy. Her hard shell was back. 'They're not coming for me,' muttered Kizzy, 'they're coming, like Prue did, for the House. None of them like me 'cept Clem.'

Three o'clock struck from the stable cupola clock. 'It's time,' cried Mrs Blount, and Kizzy fled to Peters in the kitchen.

'Hey, you should be at the front door greeting your guests.'

'I don't want to greet them.' Kizzy flung herself into Peters' arms. 'I won't. I can't. They don't like me. They're just coming for the House. They don't like me.'

'Sorry for yourself, aren't you?' said Peters.

'I tell you they don't.' Kizzy was frantic.

'Give them a chance.'

Kizzy shook her head and buried her curls in his coat. 'I'll stay here in the kitchen with you.'

'You'll do nothing of the kind.'

'Let me. Let me.' It was rising to one of Kizzy's shrieks and Peters took her by the shoulders, shook her and stood her away on her own feet.

'Want a smack across your bottom?' He was terse, his blue eyes fierce. 'Think I'm going to let you spoil this for everyone?'

'*I* – spoil it?' Kizzy was so surprised she spoke quietly.

'Yes, you. After all our trouble. You stand up and behave, Miss Kezia.'

'I'm Kizzy.'

'Kizzy and Kezia.'

'Half and half,' pleaded Kizzy.

'You're both. That's why, though you're small, you have to be big,' said Peters, 'and I never heard that either of them two were cowards. Put your chin up,' he commanded. 'Now go and stand with Sir Admiral and her ladyship at the front door where you belong. Quick march,' said Peters.

'But they're all coming at once,' said Kizzy, amazed, and true, coming up the drive was a procession, boys first, girls after, all the boys and girls of Amberhurst school – and what were they bringing? As Kizzy stood on the steps, her legs began to tremble so much that she had to hold Olivia's hand.

In their midst was her wagon – the boys were pulling it by the shafts – her wagon, 'not burnt,' whispered Kizzy. Far from it; its blue paint was glossily new, as was its gilding; its brass flashed and its windows were clean; the white curtains were new and the window boxes filled with earth. Prudence carried the kittle iron: Mary Jo the kettle; best of all, under the wagon was slung a net of hay. 'F–for Joey?' stammered Kizzy.

★

'You see,' Admiral Twiss explained to Kizzy, 'the wagon almost escaped the fire. It was smoked and blackened, everything scorched and grimed, that was all.' The boys took it out of the cottage garden and hid it in the Olivers' barn, 'And all of us worked to make it new,' said Clem.

'I bought the plastic flowers,' said Elizabeth, 'with my own pocket money.'

'My mum made the pillows and pillowcases,' broke in Carol, 'and me and Dawn stuffed them.'

'Lots of our mothers patchworked to make the quilts.'

'Mum and I washed the china with sand and cold water,' said Prue. 'That's best after a fire and not one saucer was broken.'

'Mine found new little teaspoons.'

'Clem and the boys rubbed the paint down, then painted it.'

'But Admiral Twiss did the gilding.'

'My dad put on bicycle tyres so the wagon could go easier on the road.' That was Susan from the garage.

'Mine got the bulbs, little daffodils for the window boxes,' said Jennifer from the market garden.

'The little mirror's from me.'

'We gave the carpet.'

The babel went on until Nat came, bringing Joey at a trot; Joey was wearing harness, and what harness!

His forelock and his bridle were tied with coloured ribbons: his bridle and collar were red with black facings, as was the saddle holding the rein guards. Bridle and reins were studded with tiny brass hearts and diamonds, 'flashings', Nat called them. 'Real gypsy!' and he had tied a ribbon on the whip. There was a tense silence while Nat and Admiral Twiss lowered the shafts, backed Joey between them, buckled the breechings and hooked the traces. Then, 'He fits!' the shout went up. 'He fits.'

'There's a girl,' the newest child at Amberhurst School said to her mother three months later, 'a girl who's a gypsy – at least, she's half a gypsy. She has rings in her ears and she sometimes comes to school in a little wagon. It's her own wagon, a real gypsy one, and she leads the pony herself. The pony is called Joey and his harness is red and black and sparkling.'

'Sparkling?'

'It has little bits of polished brass. She unharnesses the pony and turns him into a field while we have lessons and sometimes Mrs Blount lets her ask two boys or girls to go in the wagon and eat their lunch with her – not me, of course, big girls like Mary Jo, Elizabeth or Prue, but perhaps one day she might ask me. In the afternoon, she harnesses the pony and leads him home. Sometimes she just rides him without the wagon. I wish I was a gypsy,' and the new child began to sing, with love and longing, '*Gypsy, gypsy joker, get a red hot poker,*' and, '*Tinker Tinkety-tink. Diddakoi.*'